BOOK FOUR
THE
WINNING
EDGE
SERIES

Published in Nashville, Tennessee, by Tommy Nelson™, a division of Thomas Nelson, Inc. Executive Editor: Laura Minchew; Managing Editor: Beverly Phillips. Book Design by Kandi Shepherd.

Unless otherwise indicated, Scripture quotations are from the *International Children's Bible, New Century Version,* copyright © 1983, 1986, 1988.

The author expresses special thanks to Megan McAndrew, whose help with technical details has been invaluable. Thanks also to Kay McAndrew.

Library of Congress Cataloging-in-Publication Data
Kirby, Lynn. 1956–
    A Surprise Finish / by Lynn Kirby.
        p. cm.—(The winning edge series ; 4)
    Summary: Eighth-grader Kristen Grant fears her family's decision to go overseas to do mission work will end her prizewinning figure skating.
    ISBN 0-8499-5838-5
    [1. Ice skating—Fiction. 2. Christian life—Fiction.]
I. Title. II. Series: Kirby, Lynn, 1956–   Winning edge series : 4.
PZ7.K633523Su 1998
[Fic]—dc21

                                                    98–39002
                                                        CIP
                                                        AC

Printed in the United States of America
98 99 00 01 02 QPV 9 8 7 6 5 4 3 2 1

BOOK FOUR
THE
WINNING
EDGE
SERIES

A Surprise Finish

Lynn Kirby

Tommy
NELSON

Thomas Nelson, Inc.
Nashville

For my husband, who has been blessed
with a heart for the world.

Figure Skating Terms

Boards—The barrier around the ice surface is often referred to as "the boards."

Choreography—The arrangement of dance to music. In figure skating, it would be figure skating moves to music.

Crossovers—While going forward or backward, the skater crosses one foot over the other.

Edges—The skate blade has two sharp edges with a slight hollow in the middle. The edge on the outside of the foot is called the "outside edge." The edge on the inside of the foot is called the "inside edge."

Footwork—A series of turns, steps, and positions executed while moving across the ice.

Jumps

Axel—A jump that takes off from a forward outside edge. The skater makes one and a half turns in the air to land on a back outside edge of the opposite foot. A *Double Axel Jump* is the same as the axel, but the skater rotates two and a half times in the air. For a *Triple Axel,* the skater rotates three and a half times.

Ballet Jump—From a backward outside edge, the skater taps the ice behind with the toe pick and springs into the air, turning forward. The jump appears as a simple, graceful leap, landing forward.

Bunny Hop—A beginner jump. The skater springs forward from one foot, touches down with the toe pick of the other foot, and lands on the original foot going forward.

Combination Jump—The skater performs two or more jumps without making a turn or step in between.

Flip Jump—From a back inside edge, the skater takes off by thrusting a toe pick into the ice behind her, vaults into the air, where she makes a full turn, and lands on the back outside edge of the other foot. A *Double Flip Jump* is the same as the flip jump, but with two rotations. For a *Triple Flip*, the skater makes three rotations.

Loop Jump—The skater takes off from a back outside edge, makes a full turn in the air, and lands on the same back outside edge. A *Double Loop Jump* is the same as the loop jump, but the skater rotates two times. For a *Triple Loop Jump*, the skater completes three rotations.

Lutz Jump—Similar to the flip jump except the skater takes off from a back outside edge, thrusts a toe pick into the ice, makes a full turn in the air, and lands on the back outside edge of the other foot. Usually done in the corner. A *Double Lutz Jump* is the same as the lutz jump, but with two rotations. A *Triple Lutz Jump* is the same as the lutz jump, but the skater makes three full rotations.

Salchow Jump—The skater takes off from a back inside edge, makes a full turn in the air, and lands on the back outside edge of the other foot. A *Double Salchow* is the same as the salchow, but the skater makes two full rotations. For a *Triple Salchow,* the skater makes three rotations.

Toe Loop Jump—The skater takes off from a back outside edge assisted by a toe pick thrust, makes a full turn in the air, and lands on the back outside edge of the same foot. A *Double Toe Loop* is the same as the toe loop jump, but with two rotations. For a *Triple Toe Loop,* the skater makes three full rotations.

Waltz Jump—The skater takes off from a forward outside edge, makes a half turn, and lands on the back outside edge of the other foot.

Moves in the Field—Figure skaters must pass a series of tests in order to advance to each competitive level. These tests consist of stroking, edges, and turns skated in prescribed patterns. Sometimes referred to as Field Moves.

Spins

Camel Spin—A spin in an arabesque position.

Combination Spin—The skater changes from one position to another while continuing to spin.

Flying Camel—A flying spin. The skater jumps from a forward outside edge and lands in a camel position, rotating on the backward outside edge of the opposite foot.

Layback Spin—A spin that is completed with the skater's head and shoulders leaning backward with the free leg bent behind in an "attitude" position.

One-foot Spin—An upright spin on one foot.

Sit Spin—A spin performed in a "sitting" position, on a bent knee with the free leg extended in front.

Two-foot Spin—The first spin a skater learns. The skater uses both feet.

Shoot-the-duck—One leg is extended in front while the skater glides on a deeply bent knee.

Skate Guards—Rubber protectors worn over skating blades when walking off ice. Also called blade guards.

Spiral—The skater glides down the ice on one foot with the free leg extended high in back.

Spread Eagle—The skater glides on two feet with toes pointed outward.

Stroking—Pushing with one foot, then the other, to glide across the ice.

Three-turn—A turn on one foot from forward to backward or backward to forward. Traces a "3" on the ice.

Toe Picks—The sharp teeth on the front of the figure skating blade. Used to assist in turns, jumps, and spins.

Zamboni—The large machine used to make the ice surface smooth.

One

"Hey, Kristen! Watch out!"

Kristen Grant skidded to a quick stop, sending up a spray of ice with her skate blades. She was just in time to see her twin brother, Kevin, launch into a huge split jump only a few feet away.

"Kevin!" yelled Kristen, exasperated. "I was trying to practice my competition program!"

"Sorry, Kris!" Kevin called back.

"Sure you are!" Kristen fumed. Although they were twins and both had curly hair and brown eyes, Kristen's hair was auburn while Kevin's was more of a bright red. And while Kristen worked hard at everything she did—especially skating—Kevin delighted in playing practical jokes. Often he teamed up with his friend Manuel to tease his sister and her friends.

Kristen sighed and went back to her practice, but before she completed the routine's first jump the freestyle session had ended.

It's time for a break anyway, Kristen thought as she stepped off the ice and fished her water bottle out of her skate bag. Then she sat down on a nearby bench and put on her skate guards.*

While the Zamboni* resurfaced the ice, another skater, a girl with dark hair plaited in dozens of tiny braids, sat down next to her. Jamie Summers had moved to Walton with her mother only a few months before. Jamie was thirteen, the same age as Kristen, but she was already a champion skater.

"Hey, Kristen!" said Jamie. "Some of us are going to Dairy Haven after practice today. You want to come with us?"

Kristen nodded. "Sure. Mom's going to be late picking Kevin and me up." Then, remembering her brother's latest prank, she frowned and added, "*I'll* come with you, but let's leave Kevin here!"

The Zamboni made another pass around the rink, leaving behind a gleaming, smooth ice surface.

Kristen and Jamie were soon joined by thirteen-year-old Amy Pederson, a fair-haired girl with hazel eyes. Right behind her was Shannon Roberts, who was also thirteen but very small for her age. She had short dark hair and dark eyes. Shannon had been skating less than a year, but she was a quick study. Following them, as always lately, was Shannon's sister, Tiffany, a charmer who had recently turned seven. Her long dark braid swung from side to side against her back.

---

*An asterisk in the text indicates a figure skating term that is in the list of definitions on pages v-viii.

"Hey, Kristen!" said Amy, giggling. "You'll never guess what we did to Kevin!"

Tiffany giggled, too. "He's going to be so mad!" she said, rolling her eyes dramatically.

"Yeah! We switched the tape for his program!" added Shannon. "When he puts on his program tape, it will play 'Twist and Shout.' This should make us even for that last joke he and Manuel played on *us*!"

Kristen grinned. "And for almost running into me a few minutes ago! But won't Coach McKinney know it's not Kevin's tape?" She knew that Kevin had a lesson scheduled later that morning with Coach McKinney.

"We made sure the tapes look exactly alike," Amy assured her. "Then Tiffany switched them."

"Nobody even saw me!" boasted Tiffany.

Shannon looked at her little sister and shook her head. "She's real sneaky, but sometimes it's handy!"

Tiffany stuck out her tongue and left to find some friends her age. Kristen smiled. "That'll be a good joke. And after last week—"

"Yeah!" agreed Jamie. "The coach was really sore when Kevin messed with the tape player last week. He told him if he ever did anything like that again, he'd make him practice footwork* for two hours!" She paused a moment. "Maybe this is *too* mean, you guys!"

Kristen shrugged. "Kevin needs to work on the footwork for his program anyway."

Jamie nodded. "Yeah, the regional competition is just weeks away. I wish I had more time. I need it if I'm going to have any chance of beating Tamara Vasiliev."

That surprised Kristen. After all, Jamie had beaten Tamara, the novice national champion, at a competition last spring.

Amy agreed. "Yeah, regionals are early this year. It isn't fair—I'll *never* be ready in time!"

"Kristen's got it the worst," put in Shannon. "She has to miss almost two weeks of skating."

"Two weeks!" exclaimed Jamie, horrified.

"Only a week and three days," explained Kristen. "Kevin and I are going on a mission trip with our church group."

"I thought that trip was canceled," said Amy.

"No, it was changed from June to August," explained Kristen. "We're leaving the end of next week."

"Can't you stay here?" asked Amy.

"Surely they would understand with the regional championship coming up!" insisted Jamie.

"Mom and Dad would never let me back out now," said Kristen. "Anyway, I really *want* to go! Besides, I don't think it will hurt to take a little time off from skating."

The Zamboni finished, and Amy stood up and pulled off her skate guards. "Well, I'm glad *I* don't have to miss a week of practice. I'm having enough trouble with my program."

"You're such a good skater," said Shannon, stepping onto the ice. "I'm sure you'll skate great at regionals!"

"I see you're landing your double axel*," added Jamie, "and that's the most important thing at your level!"

"Yeah," said Kristen. However, as she headed back onto the ice, Kristen wondered if she was really so sure of her program.

Kristen had worked harder to get ready for this competition than any other since she had begun skating at age five. She didn't feel as talented as Jamie, but she felt she could make it up with diligent practice. Lately, when all her friends took a break, Kristen often stayed on the ice to work on her latest jump or spin.

She felt especially good about her new programs for this year's regional championship. At her level she competed with two programs: a short program in which certain moves were required and a longer "artistic" program. Kristen's short program had a lively Irish theme that was a lot of fun to perform. However, her long program was a real masterpiece! She felt that it was the most beautiful program she had ever performed.

After warming up again, Kristen went to work on jumps. There were two jump combinations in her long program, as well as several double jumps. But the most difficult for Kristen was the double axel.

Kristen performed a few backward crossovers* to set up the jump, then stepped onto the forward outside edge* of her left skate. She launched into the jump and rotated two and a half times before she landed smoothly on her right outside edge, traveling backward. *Perfect!*

Before she could congratulate herself, she heard "Twist and Shout" playing on the tape player. She turned to see Kevin skating toward Coach McKinney, looking confused, while Amy and Shannon were exploding with laughter on the other side of the rink. Coach McKinney didn't seem to notice the girls. He was clearly scolding Kevin, who listened, red-faced. He managed to glance up with anger at Kristen as she skated by.

Kristen joined Amy and Shannon at the boards*. "Kevin thinks *I* did it!"

"Sorry, Kristen!" apologized Amy. "But it *was* funny! Did you see the look on his face when the coach turned on his tape?"

"I know," Shannon said, giggling. "We got him good!"

"Just remember," warned Kristen as she tied back her long, curly red hair, "Kevin will probably get you back worse!"

"But he thinks *you* switched the tape!" Amy reminded her.

"Not for long! I have to live with him *and* my parents," Kristen said, obviously annoyed.

"You're not telling on us, are you?" asked Amy.

"I'm not being grounded for you guys. If it comes up, you'd better watch out!" Kristen said. Then she glanced at the clock. "Oh, no! My lesson. Gotta go."

❄ ❄ ❄ ❄ ❄

Coach Elena Grischenko, an elegant woman with chin-length dark blond hair and piercing blue eyes, was already waiting for Kristen. "You are late!" she commented in her thick Ukrainian accent.

"I'm sorry," apologized Kristen. "But I've been working hard on my double axel all morning."

"I have noticed," said her coach. "Let's see it!"

Kristen went out and performed a double axel, not as perfect as the last one, but almost as good. She skated back to her coach, hoping for a sign of approval.

Coach Grischenko nodded and said simply, "That is better. Now do the double lutz*–double toe combination."

Kristen knew that if Coach Grischenko didn't offer any criticism, she must have been pleased with her jump. She thought, *Maybe she'll let me put it in my program*. Kristen felt good as she set up the combination jump* and landed it perfectly.

After working through the other jumps in her program, Coach Grischenko told Kristen to prepare to skate her long program. Kristen skated to her starting position and waited for the first notes of her music to begin. To her surprise, instead of the *Sleeping Beauty* ballet, "Yellow Submarine" by the Beatles filled the arena. Kristen thought she saw Jamie and Shannon duck behind the boards. *Just wait 'til I get my hands on them!* she fumed.

Kristen got her extra program tape from her skate bag, while Coach Grischenko stood glaring at her. The delay caused Kristen to become extremely nervous. She blew her first move, a flying camel*, and went on to the jump combination. Now, her timing was off. She launched into a double lutz, but barely landed it. Then she didn't have enough speed to complete her double toe loop*, so she did a single toe loop*. By the time she got to the double axel, Kristen's composure was blown. She launched into the jump, made two rotations, and fell to the ice with a loud thud! There was no point in finishing the program.

Kristen picked herself up off the ice. *That was terrible. Less than two months before regionals! After school starts I won't be able to practice as much. I can't afford to take time off. Somehow, I'll just have to get out of that mission trip,* she thought. *Now, who could I stay with . . .*

❋ ❋ ❋ ❋ ❋

By the time Kristen's lesson was over the other girls already had their skates off and were waiting on her to go to Dairy Haven.

"Hurry up, Kristen!" called Tiffany. "We're hungry!"

"You mean *you're* hungry!" Kristen said with a smile as she hurried to put away her skates.

"I'm *always* hungry!" answered Tiffany.

The girls left Kevin and his friend Manuel behind and headed for Dairy Haven. Once there, they ordered and raced to their favorite table to sit down and eat.

While the other girls ordered sensible grilled chicken sandwiches, Jamie asked for a hamburger with the works and French fries.

"You're so lucky!" said Shannon enviously. "My ballet instructor would flip if she caught me with those fries!"

Jamie grinned. "That's why I like summer. I'm skating so much I can eat whatever I want!"

Amy sighed. "I can't believe summer's almost over!"

Shannon agreed. "Me, either. I haven't done half the things I wanted."

"Like switching my tape?" suggested Kristen as she gave her friends a menacing look.

"Who, us?" asked Amy innocently.

"Yes, you guys!" said Kristen. "I thought Coach Grischenko was going to kill me!"

"You should have seen her face!" said Jamie.

"I did!" said Kristen. "She was glaring at *me*!"

"Well, I guess someone was just having fun," said Shannon.

"My coach wasn't laughing!" said Kristen. "And neither was I! Especially when I messed up my program!"

"That wasn't because of the tape!" teased Jamie. "Besides, sometimes tapes get mixed up at competitions. You need to know what to do when that happens!"

"You guys didn't think about this very much," said Kristen slyly.

"We did, too!" yelled Tiffany.

"Tiffany!" both Amy and Jamie exclaimed.

"Now you've blown it," said Shannon straight to Tiffany.

Ignoring the older girls, Tiffany asked, "Kristen, what made you say that anyway?"

Kristen smiled. "Now, you have Kevin and me to watch out for. . . . Oh, my, what would happen to you guys if we teamed together? . . . Kevin is such a *wonderful* brother. I don't believe I've ever felt closer to him than I do at this moment."

There was a collective sigh at the table as the girls realized what they'd done.

"But we did get you out of trouble," Jamie said.

"Just keep trying, Jamie," said Kristen, then she changed the subject. "All I want to do right now is please Coach Grischenko!"

"Yeah, I know what you mean!" said Amy. "If we could make *her* happy, maybe we'd have a chance at regionals."

Kristen shook her head. "It's going to be tough for all of us. Except Jamie! I'll bet she makes it all the way to nationals this year!"

"I'll bet you do, Jamie," agreed Amy. "You won the regional championship at the novice level last fall."

Jamie sighed. "Yeah, but I skated so badly at the sectional championships I didn't qualify for nationals. And last year I competed in a different region. This year I'm in the same region as Teri Hall and Tamara Vasiliev!"

"But you beat Tamara at that competition in Nashville last spring!" said Shannon.

"Yeah, but maybe she just had a bad skate," said Jamie. "And Teri Hall is almost as good as Tamara. She competed at nationals last year."

"I wish *I* was going to regionals," said Shannon.

"Why don't you?" asked Amy.

Shannon shook her head. "Coach Barnes said she wants me to have more than one year of experience. So, she's having me compete in small competitions."

"Bummer!" said Jamie. "That means you'll have to wait a whole year before the next regionals."

Shannon sighed, then added, "Yeah. Anyway, summer dance camp is next week and auditions for *The Nutcracker* are right after school starts."

"Cool!" said Kristen. "Are you going to audition?"

Shannon looked thoughtful. "I'm not sure. The senior company has all the star roles, but there are still some good parts in open auditions."

"But if you get a part you won't have time to skate!" Amy pointed out.

Shannon looked distressed. "I know."

"But you've been in ballet a long time," said Kristen. "It's a tough choice. It's sorta like mine. I thought I could do everything and then all the dates went berserk. Now, it seems I can either skate at regionals or go on the mission trip."

"I wish April was here," said Tiffany. April Lawrence was Tiffany's sidekick. She was spending all of her summer vacation at her grandmother's house out of state, so Tiffany was spending more time than usual with the older girls.

In unison, the older girls answered, "So do I!"

Kristen liked Tiffany. She had always wanted a little sister. "Tiff, are you going to compete anywhere this year?"

Tiffany smiled. "No, but I'm taking swimming lessons."

"That's great, Tiff," Kristen said.

Amy changed the subject back. "Kristen, I don't think I'd ever want to do anything like that mission trip!"

"Why not?" asked Jamie. "It sounds like fun!"

"I wouldn't like it." Amy shuddered. "I know someone who went on a mission trip, and they had to use an outhouse! Ugh!" She made a face.

"Yuck! I'm sure we're staying in a modern hotel with bathrooms. Probably like one here," explained Kristen.

"But since the trip was postponed to August, couldn't you just stay here and get ready for regionals?" asked Shannon. "You could stay with us!"

"Yeah, Kristen!" piped up Tiffany. "Stay with us!"

Kristen munched on her sandwich before she answered. "I've been kind of excited about the trip," she said slowly, "but I wish we could have gone in June, like we were supposed to."

"Have you ever been overseas?" asked Jamie.

"No. That's going to be fun. And it's exciting to get a chance to do something for God," Kristen said.

"I don't know," said Amy. "It seems like you could wait until you are older."

"My parents have been planning on this for a long time," said Kristen. "They wanted us all to do a mission trip together." She frowned. "Now, with regionals coming up, I wish I didn't have to go."

"Yeah, it's tough to miss practice," agreed Jamie.

Kristen sighed. "If I can just convince my parents to let me stay."

Two

Kristen loved skating more than anything, except Jesus and her family. She had found that Jesus really was her friend forever when she was nine and asked Him to forgive her sins and be her Savior.

Each year when her church planned its mission trip, her family discussed how they would all go when the twins were thirteen. Kristen and Kevin listened in awe to the kids who had gone on mission trips and bombarded them with questions. The older kids told how they had helped build churches or taught Bible classes or worked with orphans. Every year the twins became more excited about their first trip as missionaries and curious as to where they would go.

This was the year and the project was in Romania. Kristen and Kevin had found themselves actually talking to each other—something they used to avoid. Now, when they could have been watching television or working on the computer, they talked about the trip. Once their parents let them stay up by themselves way into the night and talk.

While they had always gotten along, the trip had brought Kristen and Kevin together as friends, and Kevin had even started calling her "Kris" more often.

Now, Kristen faced a dilemma. She didn't think she could do both the trip and regionals.

"The trip, hands down!" said Kevin. Yet Kristen knew skating wasn't as important to him as it was to her.

Kristen dreaded talking to her parents about missing the trip. She delayed the conversation until it was almost too late to make a choice. She sat on her bed planning exactly how to approach her father with the news when he knocked on her bedroom door.

"Kitten, can I come in?" he asked.

"Sure," she said.

"Why aren't you packing? Don't you feel well?"

"Dad," she blurted out, "I can't go on the trip!"

"Why not?" he asked softly.

"I wanted to go in June, but not in August. I need all the practice I can get before regionals."

Her father took a deep breath and shook his head. "We've been planning this trip for months, and we're all going. I know your skating is important to you, but God and your family must come first." Her father reached over and held her hand. "Kitten, it is easy to have faith when everything is working on schedule, but everything in life does not work by a set timetable.

When it doesn't, that is when you must trust in God. He will help you with your skating. Now, you start packing."

Kristen sighed and accepted her father's decision. To her surprise she was relieved a decision had been made and enjoyed packing. *I guess Dad's right. Missing some practice won't make much of a difference. Maybe a break will be good for my skating!*

❄ ❄ ❄ ❄ ❄

I wish some of my friends could have come with us, thought Kristen as the big bus carrying the mission team members threaded its way through the streets of Budapest from the airport. The church mission team consisted of fifteen people, but there were only a couple of other teens, and they were older than Kristen and Kevin.

The twins drank in the sights of historic buildings and street signs advertising products in Hungarian.

"Look!" shouted Kevin suddenly, pointing to a large poster on the side of a building. The message was in Hungarian, but the picture was the same one used to advertise a popular animated feature film in the United States.

"Wonder if I'd like it better in Hungarian," said Kevin, laughing.

"The movie is probably shown in English," said their father, leaning over the seat. "They use Hungarian subtitles."

"Oh! Cool!" said Kevin. "Could we go see it tonight? We don't have to leave for Romania until morning!"

"No way!" said Kristen, yawning. "I'm too sleepy. I can't believe I'm so tired. What time is it anyway?" Kristen suddenly realized she wasn't sure of the day or time.

Mr. Grant laughed. "You're experiencing 'jet lag.' We left Dallas on Friday evening, but we crossed a number of time zones. We 'lost' several hours, and now it's Saturday afternoon. Your body thinks it's about five o'clock in the morning."

"*I'm* not sleepy!" declared Kevin, propping his eyes open. "I don't want to miss anything!"

"Wait," said Mr. Grant, "it will catch up with you!"

"Not me!" Kevin insisted.

Finally, they reached the hotel and the team members piled out of the bus and began unloading their bags. Mr. Grant helped Kristen and her mom get their bags, then turned to make sure Kevin had his. *But where was Kevin?*

"Look, Dad!" Kristen pointed to the window of the bus. There was Kevin still inside, sound asleep, leaning against the window!

❋ ❋ ❋ ❋ ❋

The next morning, the team boarded the bus for a small village in Romania. Budapest had been exciting and different, but it was fairly modern.

As they drove into the village, Kristen thought she had stepped back in time. The quaint old houses and gardens, many with chicken coops behind them, looked the same as they might have centuries earlier. She watched as a brightly dressed Gypsy family came down the other side of the road, riding in a horse-drawn cart.

There was also another small building behind most of the homes. It was soon obvious to Kristen and Kevin what the small houses were.

"Eew! Those must be outhouses!" said Kevin bluntly.

Mr. Grant grinned and nodded. "Most of the village has limited plumbing."

Kristen's face fell. "I thought you said we would have bathrooms where we were staying!"

"We'll be spending the night in a larger town nearby," explained their dad.

Kristen was relieved to hear she wouldn't have to use an outhouse.

✷ ✷ ✷ ✷ ✷

After attending a special church service in the village, the team members boarded their bus and made their way into the larger town where they would be spending the night.

Once at the hotel, Kristen ran into the room she would be sharing with her mother and quickly looked around.

"What's wrong?" asked her mother.

"It has a bathroom! Look, it has a bathroom!" Kristen yelled.

"I never thought I'd see you that excited about a bathroom," her mother said, then laughed.

Kristen laughed, too. She surveyed the small, plain room with meager decorations and feather pillows.

"I thought it would be more like the hotels at home," Kristen said, feeling a little disappointed. "I wonder if Dad and Kevin's room is nicer."

"Kristen, most people in this area would consider this a very nice hotel."

"I know," Kristen said, ashamed of herself. "But I just didn't expect it to be so simple. And the food—"

"I'm sure the food will be fine . . . just different," her mother said. "Kristen, we must be gracious. These people will be offering us the best they have, and we must accept it in the way it is given. To do otherwise would be rude. You must think before you say anything aloud."

"I will," Kristen said.

※ ※ ※ ※ ※

The next day, after a breakfast of bread and fruit preserves, the group climbed aboard the bus for the trip back to the village. The pastor of the village church greeted them with a huge smile. Through an interpreter, he welcomed them to his community and told them how glad he was that they had come.

The Grants were then introduced to Mirella, a young Romanian woman who would be their translator for the trip. She would also be available to advise them on local customs. Mirella greeted them warmly and led them to a small room in the church building where they would be teaching a Bible class for children.

It was almost time for the children to arrive, so Mr.

and Mrs. Grant quickly set up the flannelboard while Kristen and Kevin unpacked the crafts.

Kristen looked around. *Where are we going to work? There are no tables and few chairs,* she thought.

The twins looked at each other and shrugged. They would do their best!

Soon children of all ages arrived. Some were very tiny; some were as old as the twins. The room was so full there was hardly space for the Grants to walk—and still the children kept coming.

What are we going to do with so many children? Kristen thought, but she kept quiet. To her surprise, the children listened quietly while Mrs. Grant told a Bible story in English and Mirella translated the story into Romanian. Then Mirella asked the children to sing a song in Romanian.

Kristen and Kevin gave each child craft materials. Without tables it was difficult for the children to construct the project, but no one complained. And the children cheered when Mirella explained that the crafts were gifts from the church.

A tiny girl jumped into Kristen's arms and gave her a big hug. Kristen hugged the little girl back. Suddenly, she was glad she had come to Romania!

❉ ❊ ❋ ❊ ❉

Their second day in the village, Pastor Gheorgescu invited the mission team to dinner. All day, they could see the women of the village church preparing the evening feast.

"Boy, I'm hungry!" said Kevin, sniffing the food. Then he whispered to Kristen, "I hope that stuff tastes as good as it smells!"

Kristen watched as some of the women came outside with bowls of food and placed them on the tables. Soon the tables were groaning under the huge dishes of steaming foods. Kristen couldn't believe it. *How had those women prepared all this feast in the tiny kitchen of that house?*

Pastor Gheorgescu explained through his interpreter. "You are our honored guests, and we wish to show to you our appreciation for coming to us."

"These people are so *poor*," whispered Kristen to her father. "How did they afford all this food?"

Mr. Grant shook his head. "They've saved their very best for us. Be sure to show your appreciation of their hospitality!"

The meal began with a course of a thin soup with noodles. There was no meat in the soup, but it tasted a little like chicken. Kristen ate all the soup and reached for a glass of what she thought was clear lime soda. Kevin laughed at the funny face she made.

"What *is* this?" Kristen whispered.

"Mineral water!" answered her father. "It's bottled spring water that's been carbonated."

"What's wrong, Kris?" teased Kevin. "Don't you appreciate the hospitality?"

Kristen gave him a dirty look and then reached for some fried chicken. Besides the chicken, there were many different dishes, including a kind of mashed potatoes, a dish of something like grits, and sausages. Kristen's favorite was the cabbage rolls, called "samale."

"This looks good," said Kevin as he took a bite of fried meat. "Mmm, it *is* good!" Kevin reached for another piece and began to devour it. "What is this?"

"This is only prepared for special guests," said Mirella. "It is the brains of the pig."

Kevin nearly choked on his food, while Kristen tried to stifle a laugh. Kevin's face looked green.

"What's the matter, Kevin?" she teased. "Don't you appreciate the hospitality?"

Kevin just reached for his glass of mineral water as their father gave them both a very stern look. For the remainder of the dinner the twins ate quietly and did not ask what they were eating.

❋ ❋ ❋ ❋ ❋

Kristen found everything she did in Romania exciting. She was so busy she forgot all about regionals.

One morning Kristen and a couple of the ladies in the group went to visit a nearby orphanage. Martha Simms and Linda Wang, who were both Sunday school teachers from the Grants' church, had planned the trip. Kristen was pleased that they had invited her to come with them. Mirella agreed to come along and translate.

"Kristen, I'm glad you came with us," said Mrs. Simms, a grandmotherly woman. "We were told some of the girls are teenagers, and they might like meeting a girl their own age."

Kristen nodded, but she really was going to see the little ones.

The orphanage was for girls from the age of pre-schoolers to teenagers older than Kristen. The caretakers brought all the girls into one big room for a Bible class. Some of the small girls looked like boys. Mrs. Simms whispered an explanation. "The little ones wear their hair very short so that it is easy to keep clean."

The older girls seemed especially interested in Kristen. Some of them had studied English in school, and they asked all kinds of questions about American life. They begged Kristen to come see their room, and they led her down the hall to a dormlike room in which there were eight cots.

Kristen stared at the crowded room, with no private space for any of them. Her heart went out to these girls, who had no parents to love and care for them.

"Look!" cried a girl named Daniella. "Here is big star!"

Kristen was amused to see a poster of the music group Hanson taped to the wall, the same poster her friend Amy had in her room back home!

"Cute, yes?" asked Daniella.

"Yes!" agreed Kristen, grinning. Maybe girls in Romania weren't so different from girls in the U.S.!

But the heart-stealers were the little girls. When Kristen came back into the big room, a small girl with curly dark hair, olive skin, and huge dark eyes approached her.

"Hi, there!" said Kristen as she reached down to give the little girl a big hug. The child clung to Kristen without saying a word.

Kristen's heart melted. More than anything else, she wished she could scoop up the little girl and carry her back home with her. *Dear God,* she prayed, *who will help these little children? Could it be me?*

❄ ❄ ❄ ❄ ❄

The twins were tired but happy by the time they returned to Budapest, Hungary, for the flight home. The six days in Romania had flown by.

"I can't believe we're going to have real hamburgers again!" said Kevin. "I'm starved!"

"No wonder!" scolded Kristen. "You hardly ate anything in the village—I'll bet you hurt their feelings."

"Oh yeah?" retorted Kevin. "I ate 'pig brains'!"

Kristen didn't know what to say. Their mission adventure was nearly at an end, and she was surprised at how sad she was feeling about leaving. In such a short time, she had grown to love the Romanian people, especially the children. But now they were on their way back to Budapest to catch the flight home. They had one more stop to make, however, for hamburgers and French fries in a Budapest fast-food restaurant.

Budapest seemed modern and prosperous after the little village in which they had been working, and the hamburgers tasted good. Although the Romanians had spoiled them with their wonderful cooking, it was nice to taste familiar food, and to be able to eat in an American-style restaurant.

On the flight home, Kevin and Kristen talked about their trip and their friends at home.

"That reminds me, what type of joke are we going to play on them?" asked Kristen.

"I've been thinking about that, too," said Kevin. "I've decided the best thing is not to do anything! We'll just look like we are planning something. We can laugh a lot and whisper in each other's ear. They'll be looking in every shoe, under every bench, everywhere."

"That's a great idea," Kristen agreed. "Let's do it!"

As she leaned back in her seat, Kristen thought, *Kevin is really a master at practical jokes!*

Three

Even though they were tired, Kristen and Kevin went to the rink the morning after arriving home from Romania. Kristen could hardly wait to get back on the ice.

"They're back!" shouted Jamie when she saw them step into the rink lobby.

"How was your trip?" yelled Shannon.

"We want to hear *everything*!" joined in Amy as the three girls surrounded the twins.

"It was so cool!" said Kevin excitedly. "We got to visit a Romanian village and eat Romanian food. We even saw a real castle!"

At that, Tiffany's eyes got big. "Were there bats?" she asked.

Mystified, Kristen repeated, "Bats?"

Tiffany nodded. "Courtney says there are vampires in Romania, but my daddy says they're just bats."

Kristen smiled. "No, Tiffany, we didn't see any bats."

"But we saw Dracula's castle!" said Kevin.

"Wow!" said Manuel, clearly impressed.

"Kevin, there's no such person as Dracula," scolded Kristen. "That's just a story."

Kevin grinned at Manuel. "It was a really cool castle."

"And I ate real Romanian food," added Kevin. Then he pointed at Kristen and smiled. "But *she* didn't!"

"It was the other way around, and you know it, Kevin!" Kristen said.

"What were your jobs?" asked Amy.

"We helped with the Bible classes for the children," said Kristen. "They were so sweet. They have almost nothing. So we had to—"

"You'll have to tell us later," interrupted Jamie. "I've got a lesson."

"Yeah, we want to hear all about it," said Shannon. "Maybe after skating practice. We can't afford to miss any time today."

"Yeah, Tuesday the Zamboni broke down. The ice was so bad the coaches wouldn't let us skate!" said Amy. "So you didn't miss as much practice as you thought."

The kids headed for the ice, still talking about the cancellation of practice. Kristen was disappointed. She had expected them to be excited about her trip.

As she laced up her skates, Kristen thought, *Doesn't anybody care about our trip? Aren't they interested at all?*

Just then Coach Grischenko tapped her on the shoulder. "Good morning, Kristen. It is good you are back. How was your trip to Romania?"

Kristen smiled. *At least somebody is interested,* she thought warmly. "It was really cool! We got to do all sorts of things. And the people were so nice—"

Coach Grischenko interrupted. "Very good. I have always liked Romania. Now, we must turn our attention to the regional championships. You are ready to work hard?"

Kristen nodded, disappointed again.

"Good. Don't do too much the first day back. We want no strained muscles," the coach said as she headed onto the ice surface, where a student was waiting for her.

I guess the coach is just too busy to hear about my trip, Kristen thought.

"I'm sure glad you're back!" said Jamie as Kristen stepped onto the ice. "I've had to keep everyone in line by myself while you were gone!"

"That's not easy!" Kristen laughed.

"I resent that remark!" retorted Amy, joining them. "We really needed someone to keep *Jamie* in line!"

"Did not!" Jamie leaned forward and whispered, "But we've all had to keep *them* in line!" Jamie motioned toward the other side of the rink, where Shannon and Manuel were talking.

Kristen glanced over toward the two. Puzzled, she asked, "What do you mean?"

Amy lowered her voice. "You know, Manuel had a pairs partner at the rink where he used to skate. Shannon and Manuel have been practicing skating together!"

Kristen shrugged. "So, what's wrong with that?"

Jamie looked surprised. "Why, don't you know? Kevin likes Shannon. He'll be really jealous when he finds out!"

"My brother, Kevin?" Kristen sounded incredulous. "Just because he likes to play jokes on her doesn't mean he cares whether she skates with Manuel."

Jamie rolled her eyes. "Boy, are you clueless!"

"Anyway," added Kristen, "he didn't seem to miss Shannon when we were in Romania. We were too busy. I can't wait to tell you guys all about it."

"Sure, we'll have to get together . . . sometime." Jamie glanced at the clock mounted above the hockey scoreboard. "Well, I'd better get busy."

"See you around, Kristen!" said Amy.

Kristen followed her friends and began warming up with crossovers. She wondered why no one seemed interested in hearing about her experiences in Romania.

❊ ❊ ❊ ❊ ❊

Regionals were only five weeks away and Kristen had already missed more than a week of practice. After warming up, Kristen began working through some of the jumps and spins in her competition program. At first she felt a little rusty, but soon she was performing almost all the double jumps with her usual ease.

Kristen knew she would face stiff competition at regionals, and only the top four would qualify for the sectional competition. The national competitors would be chosen at the sectional competition. Kristen felt that her chances of placing in the top four were slim, but more than anything else she wanted to win the right to compete at the sectional championship.

❈ ❈ ❈ ❈ ❈

Kristen was so tired when she arrived home from the rink that she showered, changed, and lay down for a nap. *Jet lag,* she thought.

Yet, instead of sleeping, she kept thinking about the mission trip and regionals . . . regionals and the mission trip. She was disappointed that no one seemed interested in hearing about her trip. And then there was the big regional competition: Would she be ready? Could this be her year?

Her thoughts were interrupted by the telephone ringing. A minute later, her mother gently tapped on her door. "Kristen, are you awake? Telephone!"

"Sure, Mom," she answered, jumping out of bed and opening the door to get the portable phone. "Thanks." She closed the door and sat on her bed. "Hello?"

"Kristen? It's me, Amy."

"Hi, Amy!"

"I just wanted to tell you I'm really glad you're back! The rink wasn't the same without you!"

Kristen laughed. "You sound like I was gone for months!"

"It seemed like it!"

"Thanks. I was beginning to think nobody even cared." Kristen paused, hesitant to tell Amy how she really felt. "Nobody seems to want to hear about the trip."

"What makes you think that?"

"Well, every time I try to tell anyone about it, they change the subject."

"You just got home yesterday!" Amy reminded her. "Give us a chance!"

"Okay," said Kristen.

"You know, I've never been anywhere outside of the country before," Amy said. "Tell me about it."

"It was so special—the most special thing I have ever done in my life! Even the things I didn't like when I first got there, I learned to love."

"You really enjoyed it, didn't you?"

"Yeah. I wish I could go back." Suddenly, Kristen realized she meant it. "Amy, since I've come home, I've been thinking, maybe this is something I'd like to do with my life."

"Wow! You'd like to be a missionary?" Amy sounded amazed. "Are you serious?"

"Yeah, I guess I am." Kristen was thoughtful. "I never thought I would want to do anything like that, but you should have seen those little kids! They didn't want me to leave—and I hated to have to go! They needed help and I could help them. It was awesome."

Amy was silent for a moment. "What about skating?

You've been training as a skater since you were five. I thought you'd want to be a show skater, a coach, or something."

"I know. Me, too." She paused. "I still love skating, but I've got a long time before I have to make a decision. In the meantime, I can still go on missionary trips and skate."

"Wow. I can't imagine being a missionary. It's such a sacrifice," Amy said.

"Yeah, but it's exciting to be God's hands," Kristen said.

"I haven't thought about it like that before," said Amy.

"Anyway, right now I've got to get ready for regionals!"

"Yeah," agreed Amy. "And that's as big a job as I can handle right now! I've got to go. One of my brothers has a game tonight."

Kristen hung up the phone. Getting ready for regionals was as big a job as she could handle, too. Being a missionary would have to wait, but maybe she could ask her parents about volunteering somewhere . . . somewhere with kids.

Four

Friday nights were family nights in the Grant family. Sometimes they rented a movie and ate popcorn. Other times they picnicked at a nearby lake or visited an amusement park. But this Friday they were going to a fancy Victorian restaurant. Mr. Grant wanted them to discuss their recent trip to Romania, and he had also hinted at some special "news."

The restaurant was decorated to resemble an elaborate Victorian mansion. To Kristen's embarrassment, Kevin pulled uncomfortably at his necktie. "I liked Romania better," he muttered. Clearly, an elegant evening was not his idea of fun.

"Hush, Kevin!" admonished their mother. "This restaurant is known for its wonderful food."

Soon the family was seated, and a waitress dressed in Victorian costume presented them with menus. Kevin forgot the tightness of his tie and turned his attention to more important matters—food! "Hey, they have escargot! Aren't those snails? I think I'll have that!"

"Gross!" said Kristen, scowling. "Mom, don't let him eat those—I'll throw up!"

"Kevin, if you order those I'll expect you to eat them and Kristen to *not* throw up," their mother said.

Kevin weighed his options and stared at Kristen.

"Like your mother said, you will eat what you order," chimed in their father.

Kevin swallowed hard. "Maybe I'll try something else," he said, then turned to Kristen, "this time."

"How about the venison?" asked Mrs. Grant.

"There sure are some strange things on this menu!" said Kristen.

"That's one reason we chose this restaurant," said Mr. Grant. "It's an experience in trying something new, and we thought it was appropriate for what we have to talk about tonight."

Kristen and Kevin exchanged glances.

"You mean our trip to Romania?" asked Kevin.

"That was definitely something new!" said Kristen.

Mr. Grant wouldn't say anything else on the subject until after their food had been served. Then he asked, "What did you learn on our mission trip?"

"I learned to be careful about what I eat!" said Kevin as he picked up an unidentifiable piece of food with his fork. He made a face and put it back.

Mr. Grant laughed. "That's not a bad idea, Kevin. Even here in our own country! Anything else?"

Kristen thought for a moment, then said, "I learned that kids overseas are really just like us. They need God, too."

"And it's more exciting there," added Kevin. "Everything's different."

Mr. Grant took a deep breath and glanced at Mrs. Grant. "Well, that's what we want to talk to you about—"

"Going to Romania to live?" asked Kevin. "I'll starve!"

"Not so fast!" protested their father. "That's not what I mean."

"Then what *do* you mean?" asked Kristen a little nervously.

"Your father and I have been interested in missions for a long time," explained Mrs. Grant. "We wanted our family to have a real mission experience overseas."

"We would like to work more closely with a mission," added Mr. Grant. "And we are considering applying to the mission board to go overseas."

Kristen looked down at her plate. This was big news, and she wasn't sure how she really felt.

Kevin wasn't sure, either. "How soon would we move?" he asked.

"We haven't decided anything yet. We just wanted to let you know what we were thinking. It would mean giving up some things, perhaps even your skating, although we might serve near a rink," said Mr. Grant.

"Skating is fun, but I'd like to live overseas—if it's somewhere I *recognize* the food," said Kevin.

"I'm sure we can assure you of that request," said Mrs. Grant, smiling.

"Kristen, how do you feel?" asked Mr. Grant. "Would you be willing to go?"

Kristen was silent for a long moment. *It's one thing to be a missionary later, but right now? How can I tell my parents I'd rather skate than serve God? That would be selfish.*

"I guess if God wants us to go," said Kristen slowly, "it would be okay with me."

But inside she knew that it wasn't really okay. *What if God only wants them to go and me to stay and skate? What if He wants me to go later? How would I know?*

Kristen could hardly believe what was happening. Surely, her parents weren't *really* thinking of moving overseas.

She started considering everything her parents had said. *Dad would have to give up his job, and we would all have to learn to speak a new language. And what about school? Of course, we could have school at home like before, but there wouldn't be any homeschool groups or activities.*

But the worst thing is I'd have to give up skating—just now when I'm really skating well. It's unfair to ask me to give it up now. Training overseas wouldn't be the same. Don't they understand how much skating means to me?

"Kristen, are you all right?" asked their mother gently. "You're awfully quiet."

"I'm fine." Kristen forced a smile. *Would God really ask me to give up skating to serve Him?*

✽ ✽ ✽ ✽ ✽

That night, Kristen went straight to her room and right to bed. She usually read a chapter in her Bible before going to sleep. Tonight, however, her mind wouldn't focus on what she was reading. Finally, she put down her Bible.

Kristen looked above the dresser at the case her father had built to hold all her awards. When he first made it, she never thought it would be so full. She stared proudly at the case as she remembered how, after her last competition, her father had joked that she would just have to stop winning because the case was getting too small to hold all her medals.

As she drifted off to sleep, Kristen wondered if there would ever be any medals to add to the collection, or if her skating career would soon be over.

Five

"Why can't we tell anyone about going overseas?" Kevin asked Mrs. Grant as she drove the twins to the rink on Monday morning. "I want to tell Manuel we're going to live in Romania—with Dracula and bats. He'll be so jealous!"

Kristen just rolled her eyes. "There's no such—"

"No such person as Dracula," Kevin said as he finished her sentence. "Would you stop telling everyone that? It's ruining my reputation."

Mrs. Grant chuckled. "Back to the subject, kids. We don't want anyone to be jealous. Also, we may not be going anywhere, but if we do go somewhere it probably won't be Romania."

"Besides," said Kristen, "right now we need to get ready for regionals."

"I *am* ready for regionals!" insisted Kevin.

"Oh, *really*? What about your footwork? I heard

Coach McKinney tell you if it didn't get better, he was going to make you practice all day on Saturday!"

"Oh, that!" retorted Kevin. "My footwork is fine—I just got tripped up in my lesson."

Kristen nodded smugly. "Bet you can't do it this morning!"

"Bet I can!"

"Okay, you two!" said Mrs. Grant. "Here we are. Have a good practice, and *behave*! I'll see you in a couple of hours."

❄ ❄ ❄ ❄ ❄

Most of the other kids were already on the ice when Kristen and Kevin arrived. Kristen noticed that Shannon and Manuel were skating together. She caught her breath and looked at her brother. What would Kevin think about that? Although Manuel was a much more advanced skater than Shannon, her tiny build and beautiful posture made her a good choice for pair skating. They were only skating around the ice together, but they looked very elegant.

As she watched, Manuel lifted Shannon into the air, turned, and set her gently back on the ice. Kristen wondered if their coaches saw them. She knew that pair lifts weren't allowed without a coach's permission.

Kevin didn't seem to notice Manuel and Shannon, so Kristen said nothing. She sat down and began putting on her skates.

"We thought you'd never get here!" exclaimed Jamie, coming into the lobby with Amy and Shannon.

"Did you see Shannon and Manuel?" asked Amy. "They're doing lifts now!"

Kevin said nothing, but his face turned red and he took longer than usual to finish lacing his skates.

"Does Coach Barnes know?" teased Kristen.

"It was no big deal!" complained Shannon. "Manuel only lifted me a few inches off the ice. I can *jump* higher than that!"

"It's dangerous," said Kevin. "Maybe you shouldn't be skating with Manuel!"

Shannon and the other girls stared at Kevin in surprise. "Why not? We're just having fun."

"Well, I thought you were thinking about doing pairs," said Kevin, standing up to leave, "but not with Manuel." Kevin turned and walked off, and the girls looked at one another in amazement.

"I've never heard Kevin sound like that," said Kristen in a low voice.

Jamie looked smug. "He's jealous!"

Shannon shrugged. "He can't tell me who I can skate with!"

"Kevin will forget all about it before long," said Kristen, but inside she felt that something was bothering her brother. *I'll ask him later,* she thought.

"Anyway, there are more important things to worry about right now," said Amy. "School starts next week. Then we won't have as much time to practice."

"And regionals are only four weeks from Friday!" Jamie reminded them. "I hope I can beat Tamara!"

Amy shook her head. "With all the competitors at intermediate level, I'll be happy just to skate well."

"Don't worry!" said Kristen. "You're a good skater. I'm just hoping I can get my double axel ready in time."

"I wish I were going," said Shannon sadly.

"Maybe you could come just to watch!" suggested Jamie. "That way we could all be together!"

Shannon's dark eyes lit up. "That'd be cool!"

"Ask if you can come with us," offered Amy.

"Thanks! I will," said Shannon, looking more cheerful.

The next session started, and the girls headed back to the ice. Kristen had a lesson scheduled for later in the morning, so after her warmup she got right to work. She wanted her program for the competition to be perfect. If she had to give up skating, she wanted at least to end her skating career with an important win.

This morning her double axel jump was not going well. Kristen's timing was still off from having missed more than a week of practice. She did a few backward crossovers, stepped onto her left blade, and launched into the jump. One, two rotations—then, crash! Kristen sat on the ice, discouraged. The double axel required two and a half rotations, but for some reason she could not seem to get more than two rotations before she fell.

"Pull in your arms more!" Kristen turned to see Coach Grischenko skating toward her, frowning slightly. "You need to be very tight in the air."

Kristen picked herself up off the ice and faced her coach. "I just can't seem to get it—"

The coach nodded. "Try again."

After Kristen made several more attempts, Coach Grischenko shook her head. "No good today. Wait until tomorrow to work on it."

"But I can't afford to waste a day of practice," protested Kristen.

"Never mind," said the coach. "You will get it. But if not, you will still skate a beautiful program."

"But I can't win without a double axel!"

"Maybe you can, maybe not." Coach Grischenko shrugged. "Most important thing is to skate well."

Doesn't she even care how I place in the competition? thought Kristen hopelessly.

"It is time for your lesson." The coach skated over to the tape player, calling out, "Get ready for your long program. For now, keep the double axel out."

Kristen skated into position and took a deep breath. This time she was determined to skate a good program, and no matter what the coach said, she was going to put in the double axel!

The music began, and Kristen put her whole heart into skating every element as beautifully and perfectly as possible. The program went fairly well until time for the double axel. Kristen launched into the jump with as much energy and strength as she could muster, but once again she found herself sprawled across the ice. Discouraged, she was tempted to stop and start over.

"Finish your program!" her coach shouted.

Kristen picked herself up off the ice and continued,

but after the fall her concentration and timing were off. The music seemed to last forever. Kristen was glad when she took her final position.

Before Coach Grischenko could say anything, Kristen blurted out, "I'm sorry, Coach. That was so sloppy. I shouldn't have tried the double axel. I skated the whole program too slow, and I didn't have enough speed for my jumps—"

The coach listened without even nodding. Finally, she interrupted. "Yes, you should work on those things. And when I say leave something out, leave it out. But it was not a bad performance. You are being too hard on yourself."

Kristen was surprised. Coach Grischenko usually demanded perfection from her students. *Why isn't she being more critical? Doesn't she think I can win?*

"I want everything to be perfect!" insisted Kristen.

Coach Grischenko gave her a searching look. "It is not possible to be always perfect, Kristen." She sighed. "You will only be disappointed."

Kristen listened, stunned. *Coach Grischenko thinks I don't even have a chance,* she thought.

Six

The first day of school arrived too early for Kristen. *I wonder where I'll go to school next year?* she thought as she got ready for classes.

As usual, the first day was hectic. Kristen and Kevin arrived early to get their schedules.

"Hi, Kristen!" called Amy, who had already received her schedule. "Can you believe we're in eighth grade? Hey, look. I got Miss Norman for French class."

"Great!" answered Kristen. "I hope we'll be in the same class."

"French!" scoffed Kevin. "I'm taking Spanish—now that's a *real* language!"

"French is beautiful!" defended Kristen. "Besides, we're all hoping to be in the same class."

Shannon received her schedule and shook her head. "I have French second period instead of third. But I've got English with Amy."

"I'm keeping my fingers crossed," said Kristen. She moved up in line and received her schedule. After examining it, she looked up, disappointed. "I've got French fifth period! But I've got lunch with both of you."

They heard Kevin say in a loud voice, "French? But I signed up for Spanish!" He walked up to the girls with his schedule and a scowl on his face. "I can't believe they put me in French! The Spanish classes were all full." He shook his head. "I don't want to take French!"

Kristen looked over his shoulder and gasped. "You've got French fifth period—with me!"

Kevin moaned, "Oh, no, that's even worse!"

"Like I'm happy about it!" complained Kristen.

"Look at it this way, you guys!" said Amy. "We can all practice our French together!"

Kristen and Kevin looked at each other and groaned. Getting in the same French class was a real bummer!

❅ ❆ ❅ ❆ ❅

"Pizza!" exclaimed Amy when the girls met in the school lunch line that day. "I hope it's good! I'm hungry!"

"It's not any better than last year. In fact, maybe it *is* last year's!" said Shannon, and they all laughed.

"I'm glad we all got the same lunch period!" said Kristen as she picked up her lunch tray and headed for a table. "It's too bad Jamie isn't here."

"Yeah. Sometimes I wish I attended a private school like Jamie," said Amy.

"Not me," said Shannon.

Just as the girls started to sit down, they heard Kevin. "Hey, girls, *I'm* here! Now I can have lunch with you guys every day."

"Oh, no!" groaned Kristen, while Amy and Shannon giggled. "Are you sure you got the right schedule?"

"Yep!" said Kevin.

"Let me see it!" said Kristen.

"Nope," he said as he pulled out a chair and started to sit down. Then he saw Manuel and a group of guys on the other side of the cafeteria. "Sorry, I gotta go. . . . But I'll be back with reinforcements! . . . Oh, Kris, did you take care of that matter we discussed?"

"Yeah, I did," she answered.

Kevin winked at her. "So it's today?"

"Yeah," she said, and Kevin laughed and headed for the table where his friends were sitting.

Shannon and Amy looked at each other.

"What are you two planning?" Amy asked.

"Nothing to do with *switching tapes,*" said Kristen mysteriously.

"Uh-oh!" the girls said in unison.

Kristen smiled and changed the subject. "Can you believe it? Now they can pester us at the rink *and* the school cafeteria every day!" However, Shannon and Amy didn't seem to be paying any attention to her. They were looking at the guys.

"They're not really so bad," said Amy.

"Yeah, it's been fun skating with Manuel," said Shannon. "I kind of like pair skating."

Amy shook her head. "Kevin is *really* jealous."

"Yeah," agreed Kristen. "I've never seen him so annoyed as when he saw you skating with Manuel."

Shannon blushed. "Coach Barnes said I'd make a good pairs skater." Shannon sighed. "But my parents think I'm already doing too much, without adding pair skating."

Amy frowned. "Then you just have to prove you can do it all."

"Maybe you shouldn't ask to compete until after the ballet," Kristen said. "It's hard to do everything."

Shannon looked at Kristen hopelessly. "They also think pair skating is dangerous."

"Well, it can be," agreed Kristen. "Especially if you practice lifts without a coach!"

Shannon looked embarrassed. "Yeah, I know," she admitted. "But Manuel and I are just having fun. Do you think I should skate pairs with Kevin?"

"Did you tell him you would?" asked Kristen.

"Sorta," said Shannon. "But he didn't seem very interested until Manuel asked me."

"It's really up to the coach, Shannon. But if you make a promise, you shouldn't break it," Kristen said.

"Yeah, but I didn't promise . . . and he's the one who dropped the subject—" said Shannon.

Amy interrupted. "You know that new guy over there with Kevin and Manuel—he's cute."

"He's not new. That's Eric. But he's changed," said Shannon.

"Yeah," said Kristen. "They've all changed—and for the better."

"I hope they can't read lips!" said Amy.

The girls laughed as they glanced toward the boys.

❋ ❋ ❋ ❋ ❋

The next morning, Kristen arrived at the rink ready to tackle her double axel. She was determined to get it consistent before the regional competition. Kristen's lesson with Coach Grischenko was right after Jamie's. During practice, she intended to work hard and prove to her coach that she was capable of being a winning skater.

However, over and over Kristen fell on the jump. By the time Coach Grischenko signaled to her that it was time for her lesson, Kristen felt bruised and shaken. She wondered how she would even manage to skate.

The coach folded her arms and looked at her, making Kristen feel uncomfortable. "I have told you the double axel is not so important as you think," said the coach sternly. "Why do you not listen?"

Kristen hung her head. "I know I can get it."

Coach Grischenko shook her head. "You are learning to do it badly. It is harder to break bad habits than make new ones. You may practice the jump for ten minutes a day—no more! Do you understand?"

"Yes, ma'am," Kristen murmured. *How does she expect me to have this jump ready for the competition if she won't even let me practice?* she thought angrily.

"Now, let's work on your program," said Coach

Grischenko. "Get into position and I'll start the tape."

Reluctantly, Kristen skated to the center of the ice and took her starting position—although she already felt too tired and sore to skate. Coach Grischenko was always strict and demanding, but she seemed especially so today. Kristen wondered why.

After her lesson, Kristen skated over to the side to take a short break. As she reached for her water bottle, Jamie joined her. "Was the coach a real grouch in your lesson?" Jamie asked.

Kristen nodded. "She was pretty grumpy."

"That's how she was in my lesson, too," said Jamie. "She blew up when I tried a triple loop* in my program!"

Kristen looked puzzled. "I thought you were having trouble with that jump."

"Yeah, I know. But by regionals I'll be nailing it!" Jamie scowled. "That is, if the coach will let me put it in!"

"Jamie, you'd better do what she says—"

Jamie shook her head. "I guess you're right. But I think she'll change her mind if I start landing the jump. Then again, last time if I hadn't listened I'd have lost."

"Well, just don't get the coach mad again," begged Kristen. "I have to take lessons from her, too!"

"Sorry!" Jamie grinned. "Was she a real bear?"

"Grrrr!" said Kristen, making a fierce face.

Jamie laughed. "I don't know what I'd do without you, Kristen!"

❋ ❋ ❋ ❋ ❋

"I must have the meanest teacher alive for social studies!" complained Amy as she joined the group for lunch. "It's only the second day of school, and we have twenty pages to read for tomorrow; and there's a test on Friday!"

Kristen nodded. "Mrs. Tyrone?"

"How'd you know?" asked Amy.

"I had her for seventh grade social studies last year. She's got a reputation for being tough. I'm glad I didn't get her again this year, but I sure learned a lot—even though I really didn't want to," Kristen said. The girls all laughed. "How'd you guys like French class?"

"I like it. Miss Norman seems nice," said Amy.

Shannon agreed. "Yeah."

"I can't wait until we can speak French to each other," said Amy. "No one will know what we're saying."

"Except Kevin," Shannon reminded her.

"And Jamie," put in Kristen. "No, wait! I think Jamie's taking German."

"Have you guys noticed how Jamie's been bossing everyone around at practice?" asked Amy.

Kristen shrugged. "Well, she is an awfully good skater. Better than any of us."

"She may not be around much longer, anyway," said Amy. "I overheard Coach Grischenko talking. Jamie might go to Colorado to train."

"But she just moved here," said Kristen.

"I'm just telling you what I heard," said Amy. "I'll bet she thinks she's too good to train here anymore."

"Well, she *was* pretty mad at Coach Grischenko this

49

morning," said Kristen. "But I don't think she'd leave. After all, Coach Grischenko is one of the best coaches in the country."

"Amy, you overhear everything! Why don't we just ask Jamie about it," suggested Shannon.

Amy shook her head. "I wasn't supposed to hear anything. We might get Coach Grischenko mad at us."

"There has to be a good explanation," said Kristen. "Besides, what has you so angry with Jamie?"

"I just don't like her telling me how to skate," complained Amy. "That's why I have a coach."

"You know," said Kristen, "Jamie always says what she thinks. She's just trying to be helpful."

"Well, I wish she would help someone else."

Kristen finished her lunch, unhappy that her friends weren't getting along. *I guess I'd better talk to Jamie.* She sighed. *Why do I always have to be the peacemaker?*

❅ ❆ ❄ ❆ ❅

By that evening, Kristen had a load of homework and a load of problems. Besides worrying about moving overseas and preparing for regionals, she felt she needed to help her friends solve all their problems, too.

Dear God, she prayed, *how can I help everybody with their problems when I can't solve my own?*

Seven

"Hi, Kristen!" Jamie said as she looked up from lacing her skates and saw Kristen walking into the rink's lobby.

"Hi, Jamie!" Kristen sat on a bench next to her and began pulling skates out of her bag. "What's new?" she asked, hoping Jamie might let some information slip about going to train in Colorado.

"Not much," replied Jamie. "Just trying to get my programs ready for regionals, same as you."

"You don't have anything to worry about," said Kristen.

"Maybe not," said Jamie, "but this is going to be a tough competition. And my triples aren't going so well right now."

"My triples aren't going at all! Maybe if I was training in one of those top training centers, I would be doing triple axels* by now!" Kristen said, hoping Jamie would take the hint.

But Jamie didn't seem to notice. She just laughed, then said, "You'll be doing triples soon, at the rate you're going."

Kristen sighed. *No news there!* "In the meantime, I've got to get this double axel! I don't know why I can't land it. Sometimes it's really good, and other days all I do is fall!"

"It just takes time," Jamie assured her.

"Time is something I don't have," said Kristen. *If I move overseas, I might never get my double axel . . . or learn triple jumps!*

"Hi, you guys!" said Shannon, coming in along with Amy. They sat down and began putting on their skates. "Ready for a morning of bumps and bruises?"

"You can say that again!" said Kristen.

"Why don't we have a contest," suggested Jamie with a grin, "to see who has the most bruises after the session?"

"Oh, no!" protested Amy. "I get enough bruises already without *trying* to get more!"

"We could help!" suggested Kevin, showing up with Manuel. The two of them were ready to get on the ice.

"No, thanks!" said all the girls at once.

"We can collect bruises just fine by ourselves!" said Kristen.

"Unless you're planning to do some pair skating," said Jamie, with a glance toward Shannon.

Shannon blushed, but Manuel said, "How about it, Shannon? Do you want to try that new move we were working on?"

"When do you two work on these moves?" asked Kevin.

Shannon and Manuel just looked at him blankly. "I don't know if I'll have time today, Manuel," she said, ignoring Kevin's remark. "I've got to get ready for my lesson this morning."

"Maybe next time, then." Manuel gave Kevin a funny look and headed for the ice, along with the other kids.

"You better watch it, Kevin," whispered Kristen to her brother. "Shannon and Manuel are getting annoyed with your remarks."

"Well, she shouldn't be pair skating," said Kevin. "It's too dangerous!"

"You are jealous!" Kristen accused him. "You'd rather skate pairs with her yourself."

Kevin looked directly at his sister, but didn't say anything.

"Did she promise you she'd skate pairs with you?"

Kevin looked down. "We talked about it. I thought we had an understanding. I was looking forward to it when we came back from our trip. By then, she was skating with Manuel."

"That wasn't right, Kevin," Kristen said.

"Thanks. But there's nothing I can do now," Kevin said.

"Maybe not, but it makes me mad. They shouldn't treat you like that!"

Kevin smiled at Kristen and then turned and followed the others to the ice.

✽ ✽ ✽ ✽ ✽

In spite of what Coach Grischenko said about practicing the double axel, Kristen knew she just had to get that jump. After warming up, Kristen began working on her double axel. Yet time after time she landed in an awkward sprawl! Ice coated her tights, and her practice dress was soaking wet.

Kristen was getting ready to try the jump once more when she was stopped by the sharp Ukrainian accent of her coach. "I said ten minutes a day!"

"I'm sorry," pleaded Kristen. "I lost track of the time. And I was really close to landing it!"

"Falling over and over is not the best way to practice *landing*," Coach Grischenko sternly reminded her. "I want to see your program, right now, *without* a double axel."

Kristen reluctantly took her position and waited for the music to begin. *I'll never even place with this program!*

✽ ✽ ✽ ✽ ✽

Kristen stared at the food on her plate and poked it with her fork. She didn't really feel like eating, even if her mother had made chicken enchiladas.

"Anything wrong, Kitten?" asked Mr. Grant.

"Coach Grischenko yelled at her today!" volunteered Kevin. "You could hear her all over the rink!"

Mr. Grant gave Kevin a sharp look and turned back to his daughter. "Bad day at the rink?" he asked.

"Well, kind of," admitted Kristen. "But the coach didn't really yell." She glared at Kevin, angry at him for spilling information. "She just scolded me because I practiced the double axel too much."

Their father's eyes twinkled as he replied. "Hmm. I thought most coaches wanted their students to be hard workers."

Kristen took another stab at the food on her plate. "Well, Coach Grischenko is *not* most coaches!"

Mr. Grant said no more about it, but after dinner he whispered in Kristen's ear: "Let's go for some ice cream, just you and me. Okay?"

Kristen grinned. Getting invited out without Kevin was a special treat. And her father was a good listener. With everyone asking Kristen for advice, it would be nice to have someone listen to her for a change.

At the Dairy Haven, Kristen ordered a hot fudge sundae, and her father went for strawberry. They ate their ice cream without saying much, but after they had finished, Mr. Grant put down his spoon. "Now, is there anything you'd like to talk about? I'm all ears!"

Kristen smiled. Her dad always said that "all ears" thing, and it reminded her of when she was little. She thought a moment before answering. "It's just that everything seems all mixed up right now."

"Hmm." Her father propped his chin on his large hands and looked at her searchingly. "Does this have anything to do with our decision about going into missions?"

"I guess so. It's just that this might be my last competition, and I want it to be perfect!"

"How important is skating to you, Kitten? You've been doing it so long, I guess I take it for granted."

"Yeah, me, too," said Kristen. "It's really important."

"And what about serving God?" asked her father.

"That's important, too." Kristen sighed. "Can't I do both?"

"Maybe," said her father. "Remember, nothing's been decided. And there's always the chance that we could serve somewhere that has an ice rink."

"It wouldn't be the same."

"That's true. Isn't that what you said when you changed from being homeschooled to attending regular school?"

"I hadn't thought about that."

"Sometimes change is scary because it's something different. Yet after a while the change becomes normal." Mr. Grant thought for a moment. "I want you to be happy, but I have to do what I feel God wants me and our family to do. Can you understand?"

Kristen nodded.

"That might mean a change, but it might not. Kitten, what do you think we should do?"

Kristen struggled with her answer. As much as she loved skating, she knew she couldn't tell her father to disobey God, if he truly thought he should become a missionary.

"If God wants us to be missionaries," she answered in a small voice, "I suppose we don't have a choice."

"I love you, Kitten," said her father. "And I know God has a special plan for you. Let's just trust Him and see. Okay?"

Kristen tried to smile, but it was difficult. *Does God care about my skating?*

Eight

Kristen continued to have trouble with her double axel, but she only practiced it ten minutes each day, just as her coach had told her. However, the closer to the competition she got, the more unsure she was of being able to land the jump in competition.

Nothing else seemed to be going right, either. One day in French class, Miss Norman spent twenty minutes drilling the students on how to introduce themselves in French. Kristen tried hard to pay attention, but for some reason she just couldn't. Then the teacher turned to her and asked, "Comment vous appellez-vous?"

Kristen froze. Did the question mean *What is your name?* or *How are you?*

Suddenly, Kevin spoke up from the other side of the room, speaking in a high falsetto voice: "Je m'appelle Kristen!" The class roared in laughter, while Miss Norman tried to suppress a smile.

Kristen glared at Kevin, hurt that he would take advantage of her, but to her surprise he just winked and continued the conversation, still in a high voice. "Et vous? Comment vous appellez-vous?" To her relief, Miss Norman turned to Kevin and continued the drill, giving her a few moments to get herself back together.

Kristen was grateful to her brother for helping her, but she was still a little annoyed with him for imitating her. After class was over, he passed her on his way to his next class. "Hey, Kris! It's a good thing they stuck me in French class—looks like you needed me *this time!*"

"Well, don't get a big head about it!" retorted Kristen. Then, in a softer tone, she added, "Thanks, Kevin."

❋ ❋ ❋ ❋ ❋

On Thursday evening Kristen found herself again advising her friends. First, Shannon called. "Auditions for *The Nutcracker* are this Saturday. I still don't know what to do. If I get a really good part, I'll have to cut way back on my skating!"

"If you get a really great part," Kristen reasoned, "it might be worth missing some skating." She thought a moment before making a suggestion. "I'd go for it. Then after you know your part you can decide what to do about skating."

"Thanks, Kristen. You're right. I guess I'd already decided I should give it a try, but it's nice you agree."

Then she laughed. "Maybe I'll get to play one of the mice! Or even the mouse king!"

"Then we can tease you about being the 'big cheese'!" Kristen laughed.

Later, Amy called with more gossip about Jamie leaving Walton. "I overheard Coach Grischenko talking to Mrs. Summers today." Amy did an imitation of the coach's Ukrainian accent. "'I am sure Jamie will benefit greatly from training in another place!'"

Kristen giggled at Amy's efforts to copy the coach's distinctive accent. Then she said, "Are you sure about what you heard?"

"Positive!" affirmed Amy. "You know how ambitious she is! She'd leave in a minute if she thought it might help her win a national championship."

"I think you're being unfair," said Kristen. "Wouldn't you go?"

"Yeah, just as fast," said Amy.

Kristen hung up the phone feeling a bit overwhelmed. *Why does everybody expect me to help solve their problems?* she wondered. *I've got enough problems of my own!*

❄ ❄ ❄ ❄ ❄

The next morning, Kristen couldn't concentrate on anything. Not even skating. She ended up having a collision with one of the beginning skaters—something she had never done before. Then she realized she had left both her long-program tapes at home. Coach Grischenko wasn't happy about it, but she said Kristen could work on her short program instead. Then, halfway through, she forgot the routine!

Shamefaced, she stopped and looked helplessly at her coach. Kristen felt like running off the ice and never coming back.

Coach Grischenko stared at her in disbelief. Finally, she just shook her head. "This is not like you, Kristen. Enough for today! Your mind is not on skating!"

"I'm sorry, Coach!" apologized Kristen, while she fought to hold back tears. "I don't know what's wrong with me!"

"You need a break," said the coach. "No more practice today. Try not to think about skating at all. Tomorrow will be better."

Kristen got off the ice and stumbled toward the lobby. After pulling off her skates, she went to the rest room to wash her face. She couldn't remember ever having felt so wretched. Her last chance to skate in a regional championship, and she was going to blow it!

When she came back into the lobby, Shannon was there looking for her. "Kristen, are you okay?" she asked, looking concerned.

"I'm fine!" said Kristen, with a pasted-on smile. "Coach Grischenko just thought I was working too hard, so she told me to quit for the day."

Shannon looked unconvinced. "Well, if you're sure you're all right." She reluctantly went back to the ice.

I've got to be all right, thought Kristen. *If I'm obeying God, things will just have to work out, like Dad said.*

＊ ＊ ＊ ＊ ＊

On Saturday Mr. Grant cooked hamburgers on the grill. It was a warm evening, but Kristen thought the grilled hamburgers and baked beans tasted awfully good. She almost ate a second hamburger, but she stopped short, remembering her mother had made a homemade apple pie for dessert.

By the time they finished eating, it was getting dark. But Kristen and her family continued to sit on the patio, enjoying a rare breeze after the hot day. They sat there watching as one by one the stars came out.

"I wonder what stars we'll be seeing this time next year?" wondered Mrs. Grant.

"The same stars, of course!" said Mr. Grant, with a twinkle in his eye. "Since we will probably be living in the Northern Hemisphere. The stars don't change, even if we do."

Kristen asked in a small voice, "Then are we really going overseas?"

Their father looked at her and Kevin and smiled. "Well, I was going to wait until we had our apple pie, but your mother and I have some news."

Mrs. Grant came and took her husband's hand. "This is not definite, of course—"

"But we have made application to the mission board," continued Mr. Grant, "asking to be assigned to an eastern European country, preferably in a city such as Prague or Budapest. That way you both could continue skating."

"This is so cool!" exclaimed Kevin. "But I wish we could go someplace 'uncivilized'!"

Their parents laughed. "The idea is to go where we can be most useful," said Mr. Grant.

"Can we tell our friends now?" asked Kevin.

"Yes," said their father. "But make it clear that nothing is decided for certain."

"It will be a while before we know if we've been accepted," added their mother. "And even then there's a lot to do to get ready."

"We know this is a big step," continued Mr. Grant. "But we want to do whatever God asks us to do."

Kristen listened without saying anything. She couldn't believe what was happening. She silently prayed, *God, what do You want me to do?*

Nine

Kevin rushed into the rink on Monday morning bursting with the news. "Hey, Manuel! We're moving overseas!"

Manuel stopped lacing his skates and looked up at Kevin. "What kind of a joke is *that?*" he asked.

"No joke! We really are!" said Kevin.

"Kevin!" scolded Kristen when she caught up with her brother. "Mom and Dad said nothing is decided!"

"Decided?" asked Amy, who had just come in. She looked curiously at Kristen. "What's going on?"

"Nothing, yet," answered Kristen, annoyed with Kevin.

"I'll bet we go to Africa!" said Kevin. "That would be so cool—lions and rhinos and Masai warriors!"

"Oh, no!" cried Amy. "Then you're leaving, too!"

"Who's leaving?" demanded Jamie, who had just arrived at the rink, along with Shannon and Tiffany. They looked at the twins curiously.

"Kristen and Kevin!" said Amy sadly. "They're going to move overseas somewhere to be missionaries."

Shannon looked from Kristen to Kevin in disbelief. "Wow! Like when you went to Romania?"

Kristen nodded. "Kinda. My parents want to be missionaries. They've applied to be assigned to a mission, but they might not get accepted."

Amy shook her head. "I can't believe your parents would be so unfair! I don't see why they need to go overseas. They could do lots of mission stuff here!"

"They already do. They go every week to help out in a mission in downtown Dallas."

"Would you have to give up skating?" asked Jamie sympathetically.

"Maybe not," answered Kristen. "They've asked to be assigned someplace like the Czech Republic or Budapest, where there are rinks and coaches."

"Still," said Amy, "you'd have to leave *us*! Tell your parents you can't go!"

Tiffany came up and put her arm around Kristen. "Please don't go away!" she said tearfully.

Kevin rolled his eyes. "Come on, Manuel. Let's leave these weepy girls!"

Kristen smiled. "Don't worry, Tiff. Even if we do, it won't be right away!"

"You could stay with me!" suggested Tiffany. "I'd share my room with you!"

"Thanks," said Kristen, touched by Tiffany's offer.

"Maybe you could stay with us," offered Amy.

"We have an extra bedroom at our townhouse," added Jamie. "You could stay there."

Kristen could hardly speak. It was awfully nice to know that her friends really wanted her. "Thanks," she finally managed. "But I don't even want to think about it right now. We've got regionals, remember?"

Amy turned to Shannon. "How'd auditions go on Saturday?"

"I won't know until tomorrow," said Shannon.

Jamie glanced at the clock mounted in the lobby. "Hey, you guys! We'd better get on the ice! We're already five minutes late!"

"Oh, no!" cried Amy. "The coach will have our heads!"

Kristen tried to laugh. "Well, that's one way to get out of moving overseas!" She followed her friends onto the ice, determined to have a great practice session.

But practice did not go well. Kristen planned to work only ten minutes on the double axel, just as her coach had instructed. However, just as the ten minutes were almost over, she managed to land one. It was a very shaky landing, but still she had landed it.

I can't stop working now! Kristen thought to herself. *I'm so close!*

For the next half-hour she worked on double axels, falling on most of them but landing a few. It was almost time for her lesson. *Just one more try,* she thought to herself. She turned to begin setting up the jump when suddenly she heard a sharp voice.

"You are ready for your lesson?" Coach Grischenko was right there, staring at her with a lifted eyebrow.

Kristen turned red, embarrassed that the coach had caught her disobeying her instructions again.

"Get ready for your long program," instructed the coach. She skated over to the tape player to put on the music for Kristen's routine.

Kristen skated into place, but she was feeling shaky and bruised. As the music began and she started skating, Kristen realized she had already used up valuable energy. Before she was halfway through her program she was tired. Her spins were slow and she made two of her jumps singles instead of doubles. The longer she skated, the worse she performed, and by the time she struck her ending pose, she was breathing hard and beads of perspiration covered her forehead.

Reluctantly, she skated over to her coach, dreading to hear her comments. "Kristen, there is much more to a beautiful program than jumps," she said. "You must forget about the double axel. It is not very important." Coach Grischenko put her hand over her heart. "What is important is what's in here. You have done the work, you have practiced all the jumps and spins. But if there is nothing in here"—she pounded her chest—"your skating will have nothing to give."

Kristen wasn't sure she understood what her coach was saying. She couldn't really mean jumps were not important. But she realized her coach was right about one thing: It was what was in her heart that mattered most—not only in skating a beautiful program, but in all of her life.

* * * * *

"I heard Jamie ask Coach Grischenko about working on her triple loop jump," volunteered Amy during lunch period Tuesday. "And the coach said that she could work on it when she went to train in Denver."

"That's where regionals are," said Kristen. "Maybe she just meant they would work on it while we're there."

Amy shrugged. "That's not what it sounded like."

"Why would she want to go away?" asked Shannon.

"A lot of the top skaters move away from home to train," said Kristen. "Like Michelle Kwan and Tara Lipinksi."

"I'm offended!" exclaimed Amy. "Aren't we good enough for her?"

"I guess we're not skating in nationals or anything, like Jamie is," said Shannon.

"There's probably a good explanation," said Kristen. "Why don't we just ask Jamie?"

"*I* don't want to ask," said Amy. "I heard her tell Coach Grischenko not to tell anyone yet."

"But we're her friends," said Shannon. "We have a right to know if she's leaving."

"Well, I think—" began Kristen.

"Gossiping again!" interrupted Kevin, grinning maliciously.

"No, we're not!" protested Amy. "Just comparing notes. About . . . uh . . . triple loops!"

"Yeah, that's right! Triple loops!" chimed in Kristen.

Kevin gave her a knowing look. "Sure you were!"

"Well, if you must know," said Kristen, "we're talking about Jamie. Amy heard Coach Grischenko talking to her about going to Colorado to train."

Kevin shrugged. "So? Even if she does, she'll come back. Right?"

The girls looked at each other, unsure. "Uh . . . we don't know," said Amy. "I don't think we're supposed to know anything about it."

"So why are you talking about it?" demanded Kevin. "Who'd want to go to Colorado when she could stay in Walton at the Ice Palace?" He shook his head. "Girls!"

"Well, if you think you're so smart," said Kristen, "why don't *you* find out if Jamie's leaving?"

"'Cause I don't care!" retorted Kevin.

"Well, we don't want her to leave," said Shannon.

"Then tell her," suggested Kevin, "instead of gossiping about it." He shook his head again. "After all, what can you expect from girls! You never know anything. Like Shannon skating with Manuel! How'd you ever pick *him* to skate with?"

Shannon looked stunned. "Um . . . he just asked if I wanted to try it!"

Kevin gave her a funny look. "Well, if you really want to do pair skating, pick somebody who can actually skate!"

"I suppose you think she should pick *you*!" said Amy scornfully.

"Me?" Kevin sounded incredulous. "Nah! She wouldn't want me," he added as he turned to leave.

Kristen turned to Shannon, who was still blushing. "Why, Shannon! You're as red as your sweater!"

"I am not! I just can't believe Kevin said something like that!"

"He won't admit it, but he is *so* jealous of Manuel!" said Kristen. "He really wanted to skate pairs with you, but by the time we returned—"

Shannon blurted out, "You don't understand! We only started skating together to—"

The bell rang, signaling the end of lunch.

Kristen picked up her things. "I've got to get something from my locker before class. We'll talk later, okay?"

"See you guys at practice this afternoon," yelled Amy.

"Not me! Today's ballet and we find out our roles," Shannon yelled back.

"Let me know what you find out," said Kristen as she hurried off.

"Okay," Shannon called over her shoulder as she ran in the opposite direction.

❄ ❄ ❄ ❄ ❄

Almost everyone competing in regionals was now practicing both mornings and afternoons. After school, Kristen barely had time to eat a snack and do some homework before heading back to the rink.

Jamie's private school schedule allowed her to practice earlier than the others. She had already finished skating and was sitting in the lobby taking off her skates by the time the twins arrived at the rink. Kristen thought she seemed a little out of sorts.

"Hi, Jamie," Kristen said as she found a seat on a bench nearby. "How was practice?"

Jamie frowned. "Awful! The coach still won't let me put everything I want in my program!"

Kristen nodded sympathetically, thinking of her double axel. "I know what you mean."

"She just doesn't seem to understand that I'm going to be competing against the best skaters in the country!"

"But you beat Tamara last spring," said Kristen.

"I've never competed in nationals, though," said Jamie. "And Tamara won at the Novice Nationals last year." She leaned toward Kristen and said in a low voice, "Coach Grischenko has been awfully strict lately. Have you noticed?"

Kristen thought so, too, but she didn't think she should say that to Jamie. "She's always strict."

"Yeah, but lately nothing I do seems to please her."

I wonder if Amy is right, thought Kristen. *Maybe Jamie is going to go train somewhere else.* "Coach Grischenko is one of the best coaches in the country," she said aloud. "We might as well be happy with her. That is, unless you're thinking about going somewhere else to train," she hinted.

Jamie grinned. "I might just do that!" She zipped her skate bag shut and turned to go. "See you around!"

Kristen sat there stunned. Amy was right. Jamie was planning to leave. As Kristen removed her skate guards, Manuel stopped to talk to her. "Kristen, you've got to tell Kevin to quit bothering Shannon and me!" he complained.

70

Kristen looked at him in surprise. Manuel was normally so quiet that the other kids hardly paid any attention to him. He usually let Kevin do most of the talking. It was unlike him to complain about anything.

"What's wrong?" Kristen asked.

Manuel shook his head. "He's mad at me for skating with Shannon! All we wanted to do was have fun skating together, but Kevin acts like that's a federal crime!"

"Manuel," said Kristen, trying to keep the irritation out of her voice, "you'd better tell him yourself!"

She could hear Manuel's sigh as she headed toward the ice. She was surprised at how angry she felt toward Manuel, but she didn't like the way they were treating Kevin. Also, she was really getting tired of trying to solve everyone's problems.

Never mind, she told herself. *If I don't get to work on this competition program, I'm going to have a really big problem of my own.*

❄ ❄ ❄ ❄ ❄

By the time Kristen arrived home, it was already 7:30 P.M. She took a quick shower and had a bite to eat. She was exhausted, but still she started to work on her homework. Soon the telephone rang. *I hope that's not for me!* she thought to herself as she flipped open her social studies book.

"Kristen, phone!" called Kevin.

Kristen sighed and slammed down her book, then

reached over and picked up the portable phone. "Hello," she answered.

"Hey, Kristen, it's Shannon!" came the excited voice on the other end. "Guess what? I got two great parts in *The Nutcracker*! I'm one of the candy canes, and I'm also in the party scene. Isn't that great?"

"Congratulations!" said Kristen, trying to sound enthusiastic.

"I can't believe I got such great parts!" continued Shannon. "But my parents want me to cut down on skating until after the ballet. Now what should I do?"

Kristen sighed. She was too tired to try to figure out how to solve Shannon's problems. What could she possibly say?

"Of course, it's only until I've finished with *The Nutcracker,* and I'm not competing for a while, right?"

"Yeah," said Kristen slowly.

"And I can make it up after *The Nutcracker.* Hey, and my coach says ballet helps me be a better skater," Shannon said. "Thanks, Kristen! I don't know what I'd do without you!"

That was easy! Kristen realized Shannon had really solved her own problem. She hung up the phone, too weary to even think about social studies. She decided to go to bed and get up early to finish her homework. She set the alarm and turned off the lights.

But as tired as she was, she couldn't go to sleep. For a long time she lay awake thinking about all the problems she was facing. Always before she had felt she

72

could handle anything, but she knew she couldn't handle everything now. Not by herself, anyway. Everyone asked for her help, but there was no one to give her advice.

Dear God, she prayed, *please help me! I don't know what to do about anything anymore!*

Ten

A week before regionals Kristen could hardly keep her mind on her schoolwork. Her teachers agreed to excuse her from class during competition week, if all the assigned work was completed before she left. Kristen and Kevin would have to do double duty on homework and skating all week!

French class would be especially difficult to make up. Miss Norman had given the twins French language tapes and extra workbook pages to take the place of the classes they would be missing. Still, Kristen dreaded doing the extra work. French was the first class she had not made an A in, and Kevin, who hadn't wanted to take the class, was acing it without even studying.

On Monday afternoon, she dreaded the class more than usual. "Un, deux, trois, quatre, cinq," said Miss Norman as she drilled the class.

Kristen repeated the numbers along with the rest of

the class, but her mind wasn't on counting. She slumped in her seat, trying to look inconspicuous so that Miss Norman would not call on her. In her head, she was landing double axels, over and over, with a perfect landing every time.

"Combien de crayons?" asked Miss Norman, while she held three pencils in her hand. With a start, Kristen realized she was looking straight at her!

Desperately, Kristen tried to remember the French response. She knew the teacher was asking how many pencils were in her hand, but she couldn't remember the French word for three!

"T . . . t . . . très?" stuttered Kristen. As soon as she said it, she knew it was wrong.

"Mais non! Kevin?"

"Trois crayons, mademoiselle." Kevin continued the conversation, rescuing Kristen from further embarrassment.

After Miss Norman moved on to another student, he turned and gave his sister a wink. She winked back. *Just when I least expect it, Kevin does something nice for me. Sometimes I can't figure him out.*

❋ ❋ ❋ ❋ ❋

By the time the twins arrived at the rink that afternoon, Kristen was really tired. She had already skated for an hour and a half before school that morning, and she had worked almost the entire weekend on homework.

Quickly, she tightened her laces and headed for the ice surface, where some of the other kids were already practicing. She stepped onto the ice and began stroking*, working up speed and getting a feel for the ice.

Only a few minutes into the session, Kristen noticed that Kevin and Manuel seemed to be having some sort of contest. She watched as Kevin did a double flip,* then Manuel did one. Next Kevin performed a flying camel, then Manuel also did one.

Kristen stopped in front of the boys with a spray of ice. "What is this?" she demanded.

"We're trying to see who's the better skater," explained Manuel.

"Me, of course," put in the egotistical Kevin.

"You wish!" scoffed the equally egotistical Manuel.

Kristen folded her arms and looked from Kevin to Manuel. "What does it matter?"

"Oh, that's easy!" explained Kevin. "We're deciding who's going to skate pairs with Shannon."

"You guys have some nerve!" exclaimed Kristen. "Doesn't Shannon get a choice?"

The boys looked at each other. "No," said Kevin.

Kristen rolled her eyes. She couldn't believe the audacity of the boys.

"Yeah, there's no way Shannon would ever want to skate with *him*!" Manuel said, pointing at Kevin.

"At least I can do a decent double flip!" retorted Kevin.

"There's nothing wrong with my double flip!" responded Manuel, his voice becoming slightly higher.

"You can't land it!"

"It's better than your flying camel spin—you look like a *real* camel!"

Uh-oh, thought Kristen. *This is getting serious!*

"Better than yours!" yelled Kevin, his face turning red. "You couldn't do the flying camel on a computer!"

Kristen decided it was time to step in before things got out of hand. "Whoa! Haven't you guys forgotten something?"

Both boys stopped and glared at Kristen, annoyed with her for butting in. She quickly continued before they could go on arguing. "Shannon's not even sure she wants to be a pair skater. Even if she does, Coach Barnes has to approve her partner."

"Coach Barnes *will* choose me—" began Kevin.

"I don't see why!" interrupted Manuel.

"Wait a minute!" yelled Kristen, loud enough to get their attention. "Why don't you prove yourself at the competition, where it really counts?"

"I'm willing if he is," agreed Kevin.

Manuel nodded. "It's all right with me."

"Then you guys better get to work!" Kristen wasn't sure if her suggestion would really solve the problem, but at least they had agreed on it for now.

Kristen returned to her own practice, which meant one thing, and one thing only: the double axel—since Coach Grischenko was not at the rink. *I'm going to land that jump today if it kills me.*

Immediately, she began working on the jump. On her first try, Kristen failed to complete all the rotations.

She landed forward instead of backward and had to make a turn to finish in a backward landing position. *No good,* thought Kristen critically. Failing to make all the rotations meant the jump was "cheated." She tried again and again, but each time she made the same mistake. Unfortunately, the judges would deduct points for a jump with a cheated landing.

Over and over Kristen attempted the jump, until the skating session was almost over. Exhausted, she decided to make one last attempt. From the forward outside edge of her left skate, Kristen launched into the jump, rotated, and—CRASH! She fell hard and slid several feet across the ice into the boards. She came to a halt with a loud thud. For a few moments, she sat there too stunned to realize what had happened.

She looked up to see Kevin kneeling over her, concern written all over his face. "Kristen, are you all right? Kristen?"

"Sure, I'm fine," she managed weakly. But something told her she wasn't fine. *I should have listened to the coach,* she thought.

Eleven

"You'll need to stay off the ice for a few days," said Dr. Gallagher.

Kristen looked at him, horrified. "You don't understand!" she protested. "I have the most important competition of my life next weekend, and I have to practice!"

Dr. Gallagher shook his head and spoke kindly but firmly. "I'm sure you'll do fine in the competition. I know you well enough to know that you've worked very hard. But you're going to have to get some rest— or you won't be able to skate at all next weekend! I want you off the ice at least until Tuesday morning."

There was no point in arguing. Kristen's aching back and sore neck told her that she couldn't possibly skate right now. The forced rest gave her time to think, but thinking didn't make her feel much better. She knew what this meant. Without a double axel in her program, she was sure she didn't have a chance of doing well at regionals.

God, she prayed, *please help me get well enough to skate my best! I couldn't bear it if my last competition was a flop!*

❅ ❅ ❅ ❅ ❅

Even though she couldn't skate, Kristen still had plenty of schoolwork to keep her busy. She had just opened her English textbook when Kevin knocked on her door.

"Hey, Kris, I'm sorry about what happened today!"

"Thanks." Kristen sighed and put down her English book. "I should have listened to my coach . . . and is she going to be mad!"

Kevin came into the room and sat on the end of her bed. "Aw, you'll skate great at regionals. You always do. I don't think anyone has worked as hard as you."

Kristen looked at her brother in surprise. It was rare to receive a compliment from Kevin—he usually turned everything into a joke. "I just hope it's enough. I really want this competition to be my best ever—since it may be my last."

"I know what you mean," said Kevin. He looked at the medals hanging in the case on Kristen's wall. "If we go overseas, it won't be the same, even if we can still skate. Kris, I really don't mind giving up skating, but I hate for you to have to quit. You've worked awfully hard."

"But you've worked hard, too."

Kevin laughed. "Me? I'm so talented I never have to work!" he said, his eyes twinkling. Then he grew serious.

80

"You know I never work at anything. That's why you've got twice as many medals as me! I wish you didn't have to leave Walton."

Kristen shrugged. "I guess I don't have a choice. If Mom and Dad move overseas, they're going to drag us along."

"Maybe you could stay here, with one of the other kids."

"I've thought about that, too. But I'd miss everyone too much—*even you!*"

Kevin grinned. "Yeah, I know. You couldn't bear to be without my charm!"

Kristen picked up a pillow and threw it at him, but Kevin ducked out of the room just in time.

After he left, Kristen tried to study her English assignment, but she couldn't concentrate. It was so unlike Kevin to show his concern for her that it made her feel even worse. Still, it was nice to know he cared.

Kristen put down her English book and picked up her Bible. She had been reading the gospel of Mark, and she opened it to chapter 10. It was the story of a rich young man who came to Jesus wanting to know how to have eternal life. He told Jesus that he had already done everything the law told him to do. He was already "perfect." But in verse 21 Jesus answered, "There is still one more thing you need to do. Go and sell everything you have. . . . Then come and follow me."

Kristen realized that she was just like that young man. She had always tried to do everything right: She obeyed her parents, studied hard, and worked hard on her skating. But Jesus wanted more from her than doing good: He wanted her to give up everything and just follow and love Him.

Kristen thought about that and she was as sad as the young man in the story. *How can I give up everything? Does that mean God really wants me to be glad about giving up skating?*

❄ ❄ ❄ ❄ ❄

Kristen missed school the next day, but she spent most of the time working on her homework assignments. She was lonely and was glad when Shannon called that evening.

"How are you feeling?" Shannon asked.

"I've felt better!" replied Kristen. "I'd give anything to take back that last double axel! It's hard to sit here right before regionals."

"Never mind," said Shannon. "You've worked so hard that a few days off won't matter much!"

"I hope you're right! How's *The Nutcracker* practice?"

Shannon sighed. "My ballet teacher accused me of spending too much time skating! And I'm skating less than ever!"

Kristen laughed. "Well, I guess it's all in how you look at it!"

"Kristen, I'm thinking about trying pair skating— seriously, I mean. If my parents will agree."

"With Manuel?"

"Umm. Not exactly."

"Who?" asked Kristen.

"Do you think Kevin might like to try pair skating?" Shannon asked timidly.

Kristen laughed. "Are you kidding? He's dying to give it a try—with you, that is! He's just too shy around you to say anything."

There was silence on the other end of the line for a moment. Then Shannon said, "Don't say anything to him. I just wondered."

"Sure, I won't say anything," said Kristen.

❋ ❋ ❋ ❋ ❋

Kristen thought Tuesday would never come. There wasn't much time to practice, since they were leaving for regionals Thursday morning. Kristen decided she wouldn't even try a double axel until Coach Grischenko told her it was okay. She wasn't going to risk anything else going wrong.

At last, it was time to leave for the regional competition. Kristen and Kevin could hardly wait to get there. Mrs. Grant and the twins left for Denver, Colorado, on Thursday morning. Mr. Grant would be flying in later to watch the twins compete.

The twins were excited to finally be with their friends. Jamie Summers and her mother had arrived two days earlier, but Amy Pederson's family arrived about the same time as the Grants and brought Shannon with them. After settling in at the hotel, the group went to check out the rink. There they met Jamie, who was practicing.

"Wow! This is gorgeous!" said Amy, looking over the large, airy facility. The rink was clean and bright, with huge windows high in the walls. A number of skaters were on the ice, practicing their moves. "I can't wait to try it out!"

"It's just a rink!" said Kevin scornfully. Manuel had not arrived, and although they were having disagreements, they always stayed together to avoid being stuck with a group of girls and moms.

"Well, I think it's beautiful!" said Shannon. Although she wasn't competing, Shannon had come with Amy to support her friends and see what a regional competition was like. "I wish I was going to skate."

"Next year!" Kristen assured her.

"The ice is really good," said Jamie. Then she gleefully added, "I've been here twice for competitions and won both times."

"Is there anywhere you haven't competed?" asked Shannon. "You seem to have been everywhere!"

Jamie laughed. "Almost!" Jamie's skating career had taken her around the country to many different competitions. "This is going to be so much more fun than the last couple of competitions, though. I've got my friends with me, and my mom, too!" She glanced over to where Mrs. Summers, a tall, sophisticated woman, was talking with the other parents. Due to the new demands of Mrs. Summers's job, only Jamie's coach had gone with her to recent competitions.

"Yo, Manuel!" shouted Kevin, seeing Manuel and his parents arrive at the rink. "I thought you'd never get here!" The boys immediately set out to explore the rink.

While their parents compared notes, the girls discussed the competition. The boys' first event was the next morning at 7:30; Jamie's was at 11:00 A.M.; Amy and Kristen would be competing in the afternoon.

"Let's go see the other rink," suggested Jamie.

"You mean there are two?" asked Shannon.

"It's just a practice rink," explained Jamie, "and it's smaller. But it has a huge mirror wall!"

"I guess they don't play hockey there!" said Shannon.

Jamie laughed. "Yeah!"

"Are you going to practice today?" asked Shannon.

Kristen nodded. "We have a practice session later this evening, and again in the morning."

"I'm already nervous!" said Amy.

"We'll feel better once we get on the ice!" said Kristen. At least she hoped so! She was feeling pretty nervous herself.

❋ ❋ ❋ ❋ ❋

After eating supper at a restaurant near the hotel, the kids and their parents headed over to the arena for their practice session. The atmosphere was very intense. Skaters and coaches went about their business, paying little attention to the world around them. Kristen's stomach was tied up in knots, her mind a blur of information. She wondered if such tension was really worth it.

Shannon looked around at the scene of confusion and tension. "I've never seen anything like this!" she whispered, amazed. "All these people look like they're totally miserable!"

Amy smiled. "Yeah, you'd think it was the end of the world or something!"

"Is it always like this at regionals?" asked Shannon.

Kristen nodded. "Pretty much. This is only my third regional competition. It's serious business, because the top competitors here go on to sectionals."

"And the top competitors at sectionals go on to nationals!" added Amy.

"But it seems like it should be more fun," reflected Shannon.

"Welcome to the world of regional competition," said Jamie, joining them. Jamie's practice session was over, and now it would be Kristen and Manuel's turn. Amy and Kevin would skate the next session.

"Well, here goes nothing!" said Kristen as she finished lacing her skates. She glanced at the ice surface, already filling up with other skaters, and took a deep breath. "The sharks are already circling!"

"Never mind, Sis," said Kevin, with a wink toward Manuel, "they'll stay out of *your* way!"

Kevin is up to something! thought Kristen, but she couldn't see any evidence. So she stepped onto the ice and began warming up.

Kristen knew exactly what she needed to accomplish during this practice session, and her mind was totally focused. Therefore, it was several minutes before she realized that the other skaters were giving her strange looks. At first she tried to ignore them, but before long she grew uncomfortable. When one young girl pointed at Kristen and giggled, she knew something was up. Then she spotted Jamie, Shannon, and Amy by the boards, frantically trying to get her attention.

Whatever was going on, Kristen knew her brother was behind it! She skated over to her friends, frowning and searching for her pesky brother.

"Why is everyone looking at me?" she demanded.

"Kevin stuck a note on your back," explained Jamie, trying hard not to laugh. She pulled off the note and showed it to Kristen. It read: "I'm the best! Stay out of my way!"

Kristen's pale complexion turned beet-red. "No wonder everyone was giving me funny looks! Just wait 'til I get my hands on Kevin!"

Suddenly, Jamie burst out laughing, followed by Amy and Shannon. Kristen scowled at them. "I don't see what's so funny!"

"I'm sorry, Kristen!" said Amy. "But it was a good joke!"

Kristen just gave them a look and went back to practicing. A few minutes later Coach Grischenko called her over and gave her some instructions. "Kristen, are you ready to go through your long program?"

Kristen took her starting position and waited for the opening notes. She was determined to skate her best. She needed to prove to the other competitors that she deserved to be out there. But more than that, she wanted to prove to herself that she could skate a great program at this competition.

One by one Kristen performed the difficult elements in her program: layback spin*, double lutz–double toe combination jump, sit spin–camel spin* combination, and then the difficult double axel! As she approached the jump, she concentrated on every detail. *Takeoff, rotation, and*—CRASH—*landing!* thought Kristen, disappointed. There was no time to think; she hopped up and kept going.

The program seemed to take forever, but when Kristen finished with a very fast back spin, she knew she had skated well. Even without the double axel.

Coach Grischenko seemed pleased. "Yes, that will do," she said. She went on to give Kristen further instructions, but Kristen could think only of the double axel.

Finally, she blurted out, "What about the double axel?"

Coach Grischenko thought for a moment, then said, "Let's leave it out."

"I can't! There's no way I can win without it!"

The coach smiled. "It is a good program. No need for the double axel. Don't worry!"

But Kristen was definitely worried. *I don't care what the coach says. She knows I can't win without that jump!*

❋ ❋ ❋ ❋ ❋

"Your program looked great!" said Amy after the session was over. She and Kevin were hurriedly lacing their skates, getting ready for their turn on the ice.

"Thanks," said Kristen. "I just wish I could get that double axel."

Amy shrugged. "I'm the same level as you, and I don't have a double axel yet. Lots of the intermediates don't."

"I know," said Kristen. "It's just that I know I can do it, and besides—" She didn't want to say that this might be her last competition ever.

Amy smiled. "Your program looks so good, I don't think the judges will care if you don't have a double axel." She stood up and turned to go. "Well, it's my turn!"

"You'll do great, I know!" encouraged Kristen. She turned to her brother. "But as for *you*—"

"Peace!" exclaimed Kevin, grinning at her and making a hasty retreat. He shot onto the ice before she could get in another word.

"Just when you least expect it," she said, but Kevin was gone.

❄ ❄ ❄ ❄ ❄

Back at the hotel Kristen wasted no time getting ready for bed. It had been a really long day, with travel and skating practice. And practice was at 6:30 A.M.

Kristen lay awake for a long time, thinking about the big competition the next day. *This is it, the moment I've been preparing for all year. Will I be able to skate the way I've practiced? Should I put in the double axel no matter what the coach says?*

Twelve

Kristen awoke at 5:30 A.M. Her first feeling was panic—she thought she had missed her practice time. Then she remembered that her practice on the small rink was not until 6:30 A.M., and she didn't compete until 3:00 that afternoon.

Kevin and Mrs. Grant were already awake. Kevin had a practice at 6:00 A.M., and Mrs. Grant drove him to the arena while Kristen hurriedly dressed and ate breakfast. Although she was never very nervous before a competition, she felt unusually calm today. Kristen realized that God had given her this chance, and He would help her through it, no matter what happened.

Although Amy was in the same practice session, she and Kristen didn't talk. There was too much to think about to speak, but both girls knew they could count on the support of the other.

The practice session went well. Coach Grischenko

insisted that they not work hard, but just get the feel of the ice. Kristen breathed a sigh of relief once the session finally ended. Somehow, she hated those practice sessions right before a competition. It almost seemed easier to skate for the judges than to practice on a rink full of nervous competitors.

Amy felt the same way. "Boy, am I glad that's over!" she exclaimed when they got off the ice. "I felt like I was swimming with a bunch of sharks!"

Kristen laughed. "I never thought about it that way, but I guess you're right. That girl in the pink dress nearly ran over me twice!"

"You, too? I thought *I* was her special target!"

"Your program was looking good," said Kristen, smiling.

Amy made a face. "I don't think the coach thought so. She had me do my lutz combination about ten times before she gave up! She told me to just not worry about it!"

"I'm sure it's okay," Kristen assured her. "She only let me try two double axels."

"That's different. Most of the kids don't even have a double axel in their programs."

And it looks like there won't be one in mine, either! thought Kristen.

❄ ❄ ❄ ❄ ❄

There was no time to go back to the hotel. Kevin and Manuel were competing in a few minutes. Although there were not as many boys competing as girls, the boys were very competitive. Some of the boys in Kevin and Manuel's group even had a triple jump in their program.

Kristen watched Kevin and Manuel and wondered how they could possibly win against some of these guys. Although Kevin and Manuel were good skaters, they didn't seem as advanced as some of their competitors. Kristen felt nervous for both of them, but especially for Kevin. The prank Kevin had played on her yesterday was forgotten, for now.

The parents sat in a group in the next row. Mr. Grant had arrived just in time to watch Kevin skate, and Kristen went over to give him a hug before joining her friends. "This is going to be a tough competition!" she commented as she sat next to Jamie, Shannon, and Amy.

"Yeah, I can't believe some of these guys," agreed Amy. "They're really good!"

The girls cheered loudly for every jump and spin the boys completed. *Come on, Kevin,* Kristen silently cheered during his performance. *You can get that double lutz! Yes!* Kevin landed the jump.

Both Kevin and Manuel skated well, although Kevin missed his double salchow*, and Manuel flubbed his flying camel spin. In the end, the boys tied for sixth place in their group.

"This spoils Kristen's plan," Kevin said with a grin when the girls offered congratulations.

"Huh?" The other girls looked from Kevin to Kristen, bewildered.

"They were arguing over who was the best skater," explained Kristen. "I suggested that whoever skated better at regionals would be the best."

Kevin looked at Manuel. "I guess we're both pretty good, right?"

"Right!" agreed Manuel.

"And Shannon can decide who she wants to skate with," said Kevin.

"I guess so," said Manuel.

Shannon turned red. "But I—"

"Maybe she doesn't want to skate with anybody!" said Jamie.

"Or maybe Coach Barnes can find someone else for her to skate with," suggested Amy.

"That guy who won first looked pretty good," said Kristen. "He's from Fort Worth."

"Now, wait a minute—" began Kevin.

"Let's go check out the skate shop," proposed Kristen. They left the boys to argue it out for themselves.

❄ ❄ ❄ ❄ ❄

Before long it was time for Jamie to get ready for her first event, the long "artistic" program. Kristen, Amy, and Shannon waited anxiously. There were seven skaters before Jamie, and they watched each one critically. The second skater was Tamara Vasiliev, the champion skater they had heard so much about. She was a tiny girl, with big dark eyes, and her jumps were impressive. The girls held their breath as Tamara skated a near-perfect program to the music of *West Side Story*.

"Whoa! I don't know if anybody can beat that!" said Amy. "She's really good!"

Kristen agreed. "Now I know why Jamie's been so worried about this competition!"

Teri Hall was next, and she also skated a great program that included three triple jumps. The girls looked at one another, wondering if Jamie would still have a chance.

The next couple of skaters, however, left the ice in tears after missing important jumps. Kristen couldn't help feeling sorry for these girls. She knew what a disappointment it was to work so hard on a program only to blow it when the time came.

"That's so sad!" commented Amy after one girl finished her program with four falls. "I'll bet she lands those jumps every day in practice!"

Kristen agreed. "All it takes is a hole in the ice to ruin your entire competition!"

Suddenly, she realized that putting all her hopes on skating might really be a very unwise thing to do. Even if this was her last competition, she had had dozens of special competitions before. And if she failed to qualify for sectionals, she was certainly in good company. Most of the skaters at this competition would not qualify, either.

Dear God, she silently prayed, *I guess it doesn't really matter, does it? Please just help me to skate my very best. And help me to do it for You, not for medals!*

Jamie's program was next, and Kevin and Manuel came to watch with the girls. As Jamie skated onto the ice, they all cheered loudly and shouted, "Go, Jamie!" She turned and smiled at them, then took her starting position.

Dressed in a white tuxedo, Jamie skated to a collection of music from 1950s Hollywood musicals. Her friends clapped and cheered enthusiastically, holding their breath as she landed each jump, including three triples. As she went into her final spin, they were sure she had skated better than anyone else.

Afterward, Jamie joined her friends to wait for the results.

"It was sure great to have somebody cheering me on! I don't think I've ever skated that program better!" she said.

When the results were finally posted, Tamara had placed first, Teri second, and Jamie third.

"*I* think you should have won!" said Shannon.

Jamie shrugged. "Thanks, but the others did cleaner moves." She looked at Kristen. "I'm glad I left out the triple loop. Coach Grischenko was right—I wasn't ready."

"Yeah, she knows best," said Kristen, remembering her double axel. "Maybe you'll have it ready for sectionals."

"Anyway, tomorrow will be the *real* test," continued Jamie.

Kristen and Amy looked at each other, realizing that their test was coming up shortly.

"I'm hungry," said Kevin. "Let's get something to eat!"

Kristen suddenly felt sick to her stomach. "I don't think I could eat if I tried."

"Me, either!" agreed Amy. "But we'll go with you."

❋ ❋ ❋ ❋ ❋

Kristen and Amy ate very little at lunch. Afterward, the girls spent an hour visiting the shops in the rink complex. Jamie found a beautiful skating dress in the skate shop, a white one with gold stripes down the sides of the sleeves and a gold collar.

"I'm going to ask Mom to get that one for me," she said, admiring the dress.

"You're so lucky," sighed Amy. "You're always getting new skating dresses, or new skates. And you get all the lessons you need. Next thing we know you'll be going off to train at some posh training center." She glanced at Jamie, wondering if she would confess her plans for leaving.

But Jamie didn't admit to anything. She just laughed. "Who knows?"

The other girls looked at one another, wondering what that meant, but no one dared to ask. Besides, it would spoil the fun of the competition to actually know the truth.

❋ ❋ ❋ ❋ ❋

At last it was time for Kristen and Amy's event. Because there were so many competitors at their level, there was an elimination round. The skaters would be divided into groups and only the top skaters in each group would continue to the final round of competition. And only the top four skaters in the final round would qualify for the important sectional competition to be held in December.

Kristen and Amy both knew that their chances of qualifying for sectionals were very slim. However, they hoped to at least have the chance to skate in the final round.

Amy would be skating in the third group of competitors, Kristen the fourth. They sat together awaiting their turns.

"Pray for me!" Amy whispered just before her turn came. "I'm *so* nervous!"

"I will," Kristen said, then added, "You'll be fine!"

Amy didn't look fine, but she checked her laces and headed over to Coach Grischenko. Kristen watched anxiously, feeling almost as nervous for her friend as for herself. Since she was competing shortly, she couldn't join their friends to watch.

Kristen had seen Amy skate much better than she was today.

As she stepped off the ice, Amy groaned, "I can't believe I fell on a double salchow!" She looked as though she might burst into tears. "And that camel spin was the worst I've ever done in my life!"

There was no time to offer encouragement. It was almost time for Kristen to skate. She tried not to watch as the other competitors in her group took the ice. It was best to focus strictly on her own program. She closed her eyes and prayed, *Dear God, it's time. Please be with me, whatever happens.*

And somehow she knew that God would be with her, no matter what happened here on the ice. No matter what happened when she got home from the competition. And no matter where she and her family found themselves. A new peace filled her heart that she hadn't had before, a comforting peace that made her sure she could handle anything.

When it was her turn, Kristen skated into position and waited for the music to begin. She glanced quickly at her coach, who nodded for encouragement. The music began, and Kristen started skating, trying to interpret the beautiful sounds of the *Sleeping Beauty* ballet. One by one she completed each element in her program, skating them just the way she had done every day in practice. Double lutz–double toe combination, sit spin–camel spin combination. But as she came to the double axel, she suddenly realized that it wasn't really important. In a split second, she made a decision to leave it out of her program.

Kristen skated on, oblivious to the judges, the crowd, and even her friends who were cheering for her. She had only one thing on her mind—God's peace filling her soul. As she came to the end of her performance, she smiled. She knew that she had skated the best that she could.

Thank You, God. Nothing else matters now!

Thirteen

"Great job, Kristen!" Her friends crowded around to congratulate her shortly after she finished skating. Together with Amy they awaited the results. But Kristen was just happy to have skated well, and especially happy to be finished!

"I'll bet you make the final round," said Amy.

Kristen knew that Amy was disappointed in how she had skated. She wanted to encourage her somehow. "We'll see," she said. "We both tried our best, and that's what really counts."

Amy sighed. "I suppose so."

Finally, the results were posted. Amy had placed sixth in her group. Kristen had placed second! She had made the final round of competition.

"I can't believe it!" said Kristen, in total shock at the news. She still had a chance to qualify for sectionals.

"Well, believe it," said Jamie, "'cause you've got to get ready to skate again tomorrow!"

Kristen realized Jamie was right. Her stomach began churning. She still had a chance!

❄ ❄ ❄ ❄ ❄

The next day was busy. The final round of both Jamie's and Kristen's levels began with Jamie skating her short program in the morning and Kristen skating hers in the afternoon. Jamie's short program went well, with only a mistake on her combination spin*. When the results were posted, she had placed third, with Tamara first and Teri second.

Her friends were proud of her, but Jamie was disgusted with herself. "I could do that spin in my sleep!" she fumed. "I can't believe I messed it up here!"

Kristen understood how she felt. It was frustrating to work so hard only to make a mistake on something easy. She hoped she wouldn't do the same thing.

❄ ❄ ❄ ❄ ❄

When Kristen's turn came her legs felt like jelly underneath her. Wearing a sparkly green dress, she waited with her coach at the side of the rink.

Coach Grischenko looked her straight in the eye and said, "Kristen, you have worked very hard. You will skate well!" Then she smiled.

Kristen smiled back weakly and skated into position at center ice. She hoped her coach was right. Then the music started, and it was time. Kristen tried to skate as though she were an Irish dancer performing in a show.

It was hard to look like she was having fun when she was so nervous! Still, she managed to perform every element fairly well, and when she finished she felt she had done her best.

"Kristen, you're fourth!" shouted Jamie, running back to tell her the news as soon as the results were posted. Her friends erupted in shouts and cheers of congratulation.

Fourth! Kristen suddenly realized what that meant. She was still in the running for a chance to go to sectionals. All she had to do was stay in fourth place!

❄ ❄ ❄ ❄ ❄

That evening was the last all the kids would be together during regionals. Amy, Shannon, and Manuel were leaving the next morning to go home. So Jamie's mother arranged a small party for the kids.

The party was simple with sandwiches, chips, fruit, and desserts served on paper plates. Everyone was there when the Grants arrived.

"Hi, Kristen!" called Amy. "Are you finally hungry? You'd better get something to eat before the boys eat it all!"

"I'm starved!" said Kristen.

"I can't believe we're going home tomorrow," sighed Shannon. "It's been so much fun!"

"You didn't even compete!" said Amy.

"I know," said Shannon. "That was the best part!"

Kristen laughed. She remembered how nervous

Shannon had gotten before her last competition. "Where's Jamie?" she asked.

"I haven't seen her tonight," answered Shannon.

Kristen felt a tap on her shoulder. Someone placed a very full plate of food in her right hand and a full glass of punch in her left. It happened so fast she didn't even have a chance to see who did it.

Amy and Shannon exploded in giggles, and Kristen looked down at the plate in her hand. It was piled high with several sandwiches, veggies and dip, chips, brownies, three cupcakes, and two cheesecake tarts. It was more food than one person could possibly eat!

"Whose plate is this?" demanded Kristen, her face turning red. She tried to turn around to see who had handed it to her, but just holding on to the food without upsetting the plate was a balancing act. "Kevin?" she asked, looking at Shannon and Amy.

Amy and Shannon shook their heads, trying not to laugh. "No!"

"Manuel?"

"No." They were giggling again.

"Then who?" demanded Kristen. "Help me with this!"

Amy and Shannon rescued the cupcakes and a couple of the sandwiches, which were about to tumble overboard. "It was Jamie!" Shannon blurted out.

Kristen turned in time to see Jamie disappear behind Kevin and Manuel. "But I'll bet you guys put her up to it!" She handed her plate to Amy. "I don't think I'm hungry, after all!" she said, grinning at Kevin.

"I know what you mean," said Kevin, looking at the plate Amy was holding. He winked at Kristen. "It might not be safe to eat!"

Amy looked nervously at the plate in her hand. "What do you mean?" she asked suspiciously.

Kevin gave Kristen a significant look. Then they both burst out laughing.

"I give, you two!" exclaimed Shannon. "Ever since we played that tape switch on Kevin and you this summer, I've had to check everything twice. I'm always waiting for the joke!"

"Me, too," said Amy.

"Yeah," Jamie added. "What can we do to get you two to leave us alone?"

Kristen and Kevin both started laughing.

"The joke is: We did leave you alone!" Kevin yelled.

"All that waiting and checking you guys did was just playing the joke on yourselves," added Kristen.

Everyone, even their parents, started laughing at the girls' expense.

"That's the best joke yet," said Amy.

"Hey, you guys, I want you to meet someone," said Jamie. Kristen had just taken a big bite of one of the sandwiches when she looked up to see a tiny girl with huge dark eyes and a curly brown ponytail. "This is Tamara Vasiliev."

Kristen nearly choked on her sandwich. So this was the talented skater they had heard so much about.

"Hi, Tamara," said all the girls politely. Kristen could

tell that Amy and Shannon were as surprised as she was. They thought Jamie was jealous of Tamara.

But Tamara didn't seem to notice. Her dark brown eyes sparkled with mischief. "Hi, everybody," she said, with a very slight trace of an accent that reminded Kristen of Coach Grischenko. "Kristen, I hear you have done well in competition!"

"Thanks!" said Kristen. "I just hope I can skate well tomorrow!"

"Good luck!" said Tamara. "I hope we'll see you at sectionals! Jamie told me you are a wonderful skater."

Kristen could feel her cheeks turning pink as she glanced at Jamie. "You shouldn't believe everything she tells you!"

Tamara laughed. "I know! She also told me *she* is a wonderful skater, too!"

"I didn't!" protested Jamie, on the defensive now.

"Just kidding!" said Tamara, her eyes twinkling.

After all she had heard about Tamara being such a fierce competitor, Kristen was surprised. Tamara was friendly and personable, and wasn't a bit conceited.

"Kristen went to Romania," said Amy.

Tamara's eyes lit up. "Really? My mother is Romanian—she was a talented gymnast!"

"Wow!" said Amy. "Romania always has top gymnasts. Did your mother compete in the Olympics?"

"No," answered Tamara, shaking her head. "They wouldn't let her because she is a Christian."

The girls looked at each other, amazed that such a

thing could happen. Tamara continued the story. "My mother began to train as a gymnast from the time she was a little girl, and she was very good. Her coach told her she was one of the best in the country, maybe even in the whole world. But then her parents became Christians. Her father had an important government job, but he got in trouble with the Romanian government. When they chose the team for the world competition, they told my mother she was not good enough, even though she had won every competition she had entered. She knew it was because of her father's beliefs."

"I'll bet she was heartbroken," said Shannon.

Tamara went on. "She was very sad, but she loved God more than gymnastics. Those were very hard times. Her father was even sent to prison, and for several months they didn't know if he was alive."

"That's terrible!" said Amy. "Did he get out of prison?"

"Eventually. Things are different in Romania now."

"Did your mother quit gymnastics?" asked Jamie.

Tamara smiled and shook her head. "No. She met my father at a competition; he was a Russian gymnast. When they got married and came to America, they began teaching gymnastics."

"Didn't they want you to be a gymnast?" Kristen asked.

"Yes. I began lessons when I was small. But I liked skating better!"

"I'll bet all those gymnastic lessons helped your skating, though!" said Amy.

Tamara shrugged. "Maybe. I still like to do gymnastics sometimes!"

Jamie listened with a funny look on her face. Finally, she spoke. "Well, now I know what I've been missing in my skating!"

The other girls looked at her in surprise. Jamie continued, "I was a gymnastics dropout when I was little. That's why my mom switched me to skating!"

❄ ❄ ❄ ❄ ❄

Kristen lay awake for a long time that night, thinking about what Tamara had said. She thought about all that Tamara's mother had suffered because of her faith. Mrs. Vasiliev had not only had to give up her dreams of Olympic competition, but her father had been put in prison!

Kristen felt a little guilty. God had given her so much, and she had been able to skate and have fun at competitions for a long time. Now, He was asking her to give it up to serve Him. How could she say no?

❄ ❄ ❄ ❄ ❄

At practice the next morning, Kristen was unusually nervous. She had a difficult time practicing her jumps, but she managed to do her jump combination and her double flip.

Then Coach Grischenko said, "Try the double axel."

Kristen looked surprised, but she went out and performed the jump. To her surprise, it felt pretty good!

She looked back at her coach, who nodded. Kristen decided to try it one more time. Again, it was good.

Coach Grischenko hardly seemed to notice. When Kristen skated back to her, she simply nodded and said, "You had a good practice, Kristen. Now, go rest."

Kristen was elated that she had landed a really good double axel! Now she could use it in her program!

❋ ❋ ❋ ❋ ❋

Jamie's long program came first, during the morning. She skated nearly perfectly, and placed second, with Tamara in first, and Teri in third place. "Jamie, that was super!" said Kristen excitedly, after the results were posted. "You're going to sectionals!"

"And I expect you to come with me!" said Jamie, grinning. "I'm discovering it's a lot more fun to take my friends with me to competitions! I don't want to go alone!"

"I'll do my best, but I can't promise!" said Kristen. *That's one promise I wish I could make!*

❋ ❋ ❋ ❋ ❋

At last it was time for Kristen's long program. She was nervous, but excited about landing the double axel that morning. During the five minute warmup time she decided to give it a try, but fell on the first attempt. Distraught, she looked toward the coach for reassurance. Coach Grischenko nodded and mouthed the words: *"Yes, you can."* Kristen turned and, with a look of determination, took off and landed the jump successfully. Jubilant, she returned to the coach, who merely reminded her of the other things she needed to practice during the short warmup time.

It seemed forever before the announcer called her name. Kristen thought she had never been so nervous in her whole life. She checked the beautiful blue lace dress she was wearing, hoping she looked the part of *Sleeping Beauty*. She quickly prayed, *God, please help me to skate my best.*

The music started and Kristen began skating the familiar program. One by one she landed every jump and performed every spin. She couldn't get too excited. "Focus!" she told herself. Then it was time for the double axel. Kristen launched into the jump. One, two and a half rotations, and she had landed it! As soon as she touched the ice, her face lit up with a huge smile. She could hardly believe it! Dimly, she was aware of the loud applause from the audience, but she couldn't celebrate yet. There were still several more elements to perform.

When the last notes of her music sounded, Kristen held her ending position breathlessly. This program was the best she had ever done in competition. She couldn't believe she had skated so well!

Even Coach Grischenko couldn't keep from smiling when Kristen stepped off the ice, but she said little except, "Well done, Kristen."

"Do you think I have a chance?" asked Kristen hopefully.

The coach's face became more serious and she thought for a moment before she replied. Finally, she answered, "What is important is that you skated very, very well."

Kristen's heart sank, but she knew her coach was right. She should be really proud of how she had skated, no matter how the results came out.

❀ ❀ ❀ ❀ ❀

As she waited for the results, Kristen knew her chances of remaining in the top four were slim. Still, she couldn't help hoping she'd make it. It would be so thrilling to have the chance to skate in a major competition like that, after all her years of hard work.

"Kitten, any performance by you is always worth waiting for!" whispered her dad as he gave Kristen a hug. "I'm glad I could stay a couple of extra days!"

Kristen smiled. "Thanks, Dad! I'm glad I didn't disappoint you."

"You could *never* disappoint us," said her mother. "Not as long as you give it your best!"

Kevin couldn't disguise his pride in his sister. "That was awesome, Kris!"

"Really cool!" added Jamie. "You'll be in the top four, for sure!"

"Thanks, you guys," said Kristen, feeling happy. Right now, she was just happy to be finished!

Kristen, Jamie, and Kevin watched as a woman carried a sheet of paper into the rink and taped it to the wall where the results were posted. A crowd of skaters, parents, and coaches rushed to see, and Kristen couldn't get anywhere near.

"I can't see anything!" Kristen complained, hopping up and down trying to get a glimpse.

"I'll find out!" said Jamie, and she ducked under the crowd. After a minute more Kristen heard a "Yippee!" and saw Jamie's head pop up above the crowd. "Kristen, you made it!" she screamed. "You're third!"

Jamie and Kevin cheered, and Kristen turned to see Coach Grischenko smiling at her. But the first people she really wanted to see were her mother and father, who were waiting just outside the crowd of people. Mrs. Grant smiled and gave her a big hug. "Mom, I did it!" said Kristen happily.

"I always knew you could!" said her mom.

Fourteen

Kristen felt proud when she saw the large banner on the wall of the Ice Palace lobby. Boldly written across it was: "Congratulations, Jamie and Kristen!" She could hardly believe it was true—she was really going to the sectional competition in a few weeks.

Her friends wouldn't let her forget it. They seemed as excited for her as if they were going themselves. And they were sure that Kristen's success meant she could stay in Walton. "Surely your parents won't make you go overseas now!" they told her.

Kristen wasn't so sure. She knew she would like nothing better than to work toward the goal of winning a national championship someday. But she was beginning to realize that there were more important things than winning championships, and she was starting to think about the people who might have won championships but chose another direction.

❋ ❋ ❋ ❋ ❋

"Let's get to work on your double axel," Coach Grischenko said when it was time for Kristen's lesson.

Kristen was disappointed that the coach didn't mention the competition, but she went right to work on the difficult jump. After a couple of tries, she landed the jump somewhat shakily, but cleanly.

"Very good," said the coach. "Next time we will work on the triple salchow*."

Triple salchow! Kristen was excited. She had of course tried triple jumps on her own, but this meant that Coach Grischenko recognized that she was ready for triples! *In a few months, maybe I'll be landing the triple toe and the triple loop! . . . Oh, no! In a few months I probably won't be here!*

Kristen put that thought out of her mind. Right now, she just wanted to skate well at sectionals. Never mind what happened afterward. She would just have to trust that God would take care of things.

❋ ❋ ❋ ❋ ❋

The girls had lots to talk about during lunch that day.

"How are your rehearsals going, Shannon?" asked Kristen. "Did you miss much while you were at regionals?"

"Only one rehearsal," said Shannon. "Madame spent time with me after class going over what I missed." She sighed. "I'm glad I decided to go with my parents' decision and not skate competitively until after *The Nutcracker.* It's a lot of work. But I still want to skate

112

pairs. Hey, your parents wouldn't really make you go overseas *now,* would they?"

"We talked about it last night," said Kristen. "They haven't changed their minds, but I have."

"What do you mean?" asked her friends.

"I've decided I want to go." Kristen could see that her friends were shocked. She went on to explain. "I've been doing a lot of thinking. Remember what Tamara told us about her family? They obeyed God, no matter what. That's what I want, too."

The other girls were quiet. Finally, Shannon broke the silence. "I think I understand." Then she looked sadly at Kristen. "I guess Kevin's going overseas, too?"

"Yeah," Kristen said.

"But we're already losing Jamie!" protested Amy. "We don't want to lose you both, too!"

"Are you sure about Jamie?" asked Kristen.

"I heard her mom telling Coach Grischenko she'd already bought plane tickets," said Amy. "And did you notice how chummy she was with Tamara? Tamara trains in Denver."

The bell rang; Kristen picked up her lunch tray and stood to go. "Just because Jamie made a new friend doesn't mean she's leaving us! I don't think anyone's leaving except Kevin and me!"

❅ ❆ ❈ ❆ ❅

A few mornings later Kristen and Kevin came into the rink to find Shannon and Manuel skating together. As they watched, Shannon performed a waltz jump* with an assist from Manuel—a simple pairs move. Kevin looked a little annoyed, but he didn't say anything.

Kristen sensed trouble brewing. "Remember, you and Manuel agreed to let the best man win!"

"But we tied at regionals!" Kevin reminded her.

"And we may be leaving soon," Kristen added.

"Yeah, I know," said Kevin, with a sparkle in his brown eyes, "but I haven't left yet!"

Kevin finished lacing his skates and headed for the ice, carrying a sweatshirt he had fished out of his skate bag. To the amusement of everyone on the ice, he skated around holding the sweatshirt as if it were a person, doing elaborate pair skating moves. Someone had put on a popular music tape, and Kevin interpreted the music, ending with a final "death spiral" as he swung the sweatshirt around him while he pivoted in one spot on the ice.

Everyone in the rink applauded when Kevin finished his "program."

"You've got a great partner!" joked Manuel.

"Thanks!" said Kevin. He held out the sweatshirt admiringly. "She's a good skater—and she won't get mad if I drop her!"

The kids all laughed at that. Then Kevin added, "But I don't guess we can compete against you and Shannon. You'll probably win at regionals next year!"

Manuel glanced at Shannon, then explained, "But we're just pair skating for fun!"

Shannon added, "I don't have time to do pair skating. I just think it's kind of fun to skate with a partner!"

"Yeah, I'd like to try that sometime, too!" said Kevin.

Shannon's eyes lit up. "I'll be glad to skate with you, if you want."

"Sure!" said Kevin. He looked at Manuel. "You wouldn't mind loaning me your partner?"

Manuel grinned. "If you don't mind loaning me yours!"

Kevin laughed and threw his sweatshirt at Manuel. Then he turned to Shannon. "Ready to go for a spin?"

"Uh, I'm not as good as that sweatshirt. Let's try something easier first!" teased Shannon.

Kristen watched as they skated together, feeling relieved. *One more problem solved,* she thought as Manuel sat down next to her.

"Just between us, your brother sure is stubborn."

"What are you talking about, Manuel?" Kristen asked.

"Can you keep a secret from Kevin?" asked Manuel.

"Yes."

"Shannon said she thought you'd understand—"

"Understand what?" asked Kristen.

"Well, Kevin would never actually ask Shannon to skate pairs with him. So, when you two were on your trip, we hatched this scheme to see what he'd do. I thought he'd see us skating when he came in and that would be it! Then I thought he'd never say anything. We weren't sure what to do," Manuel said.

"All of this was a plan?"

"Sure. Kevin's my friend. I wouldn't make him jealous on purpose," said Manuel, smiling sheepishly.

"Why didn't Shannon just ask him?"

"We never thought of that!" Manuel said. "Would it have worked?"

"Yeah," said Kristen.

* * * * *

Extra practices and extra lessons kept Kristen too busy to worry about anyone's problems—even her own. Several days later, however, her parents called a special family meeting once again. Kristen could hardly concentrate on her skating or her schoolwork all day for wondering what kind of news their father had for them.

After they had finished eating supper, Mr. Grant turned to his children. "You kids have been wonderful the past few weeks," he began. "When we told you that we had applied to the mission board, I expected you both to complain and try to get us to change our minds. I'm very proud of the way you supported our decision."

Kristen knew she hadn't really been as supportive as she should, but she kept quiet.

"I think moving overseas will be cool!" said Kevin. "Where are we going?"

Mr. Grant took his wife's hand. "We've decided to withdraw our application to the mission board. We won't be going overseas."

"Why?" demanded Kevin, frowning.

"You know Grandmother McGuire has been having back problems," said Mrs. Grant. "Last week, she went to the doctor and he's recommended surgery. It's going to take several months for her to recover, and she's going to need our help."

"Will she be okay?" asked Kristen. She adored her grandmother and hated to think of her in pain.

"The doctor thinks she'll do just fine," explained her mother. "But it will take time."

"When she gets better will we go overseas?" asked Kristen.

Mrs. Grant shook her head. "We'll see. It depends on how she's doing and what we are doing."

"God wants us to be willing to serve Him wherever He calls us," added Mr. Grant. "For right now, it looks as though that will be here at home."

"Ah, rats!" grumbled Kevin, but Kristen said nothing. She realized this meant she could stay in Walton and skate, and she wouldn't have to leave her friends. But somehow Kristen felt a little disappointed.

"Just because we can't move overseas doesn't mean we can't be involved in missions," continued Mr. Grant. "How would you like to plan a mission project during our family vacation every year?"

"Cool!" said Kevin.

Kristen thought so, too. Maybe someday she would go overseas herself as a missionary. But for now, having the chance to go on mission trips would be really cool!

"I've been thinking I'd like to volunteer to work with children. Could I do that here?" asked Kristen.

"Yes," said their father.

"I think that's a wonderful idea. I'll check around and find a place for you to volunteer," said their mother.

"There are many ways to be missionaries, and

working with people in your own town is always a good place to start, Kitten," their father said.

The family talked long into the evening about the changes to come and their volunteer work for God.

As she fell asleep, Kristen thought about all that had happened. She was worried about her grandmother, but she was excited about her family's plans to serve God.

❋ ❋ ❋ ❋ ❋

Kristen's eyes opened wide when the enormous chocolate sundae was placed in front of her. It was swimming in hot fudge topping and sprinkled with chocolate candies. "How am I ever going to eat this?" she demanded.

Her friends giggled at the look of amazement on Kristen's face. It was Saturday afternoon and the girls had planned a trip to the Dairy Haven for a celebration. Kristen was usually so disciplined that she allowed herself only a small treat, but Jamie had arranged to surprise her with the most gigantic sundae on the menu!

"After all," explained Jamie as she dug into her own huge ice cream treat, "we're celebrating!"

Kristen grinned. "If I do much more celebrating, I won't be able to get off the ice for that double axel!"

"It's pretty cool that you and Jamie are both going to sectionals!" said Shannon.

Kristen sighed. "It will be a lot of work!"

"Don't complain!" said Amy. "Some of us weren't so lucky!"

"But you skated well, too," said Kristen. "Next year maybe we'll all qualify for sectionals!"

"That is, if you don't end up in Brazil or someplace!" complained Shannon. "Can't you talk your parents into letting you stay here?"

Kristen grinned. "Well, as a matter of fact: We're not moving!"

Her friends were immediately interested. "Really?"

"My grandmother is having back surgery," Kristen explained. "She'll be okay, but it's going to take a long time. And she'll need our help."

"I'm sorry about your grandmother," said Amy. "So you won't be moving overseas?"

Kristen shook her head. "Not right now. But my dad, as usual, has another plan! He's getting involved in short-term mission trips, like we did this summer. And we're going with him at least once a year!"

"Cool!" said Jamie, impressed. "That's even better!"

Kristen agreed. "Yeah, I'm glad I can stay and skate, but I kind of wanted to go overseas, too. Maybe some-day I might go as a missionary to stay!"

"Speaking of leaving," said Amy, turning to look at Jamie, "we've been wondering when *you're* leaving!"

"Me?" asked Jamie, surprised. "What do you mean?"

"We've overheard some plans for you to go to Colorado," explained Kristen.

"We even heard Coach Grischenko talking about plane tickets!" added Amy.

Jamie laughed. "Oh, that! I'm not leaving—at least not for long!"

The girls looked puzzled, and Jamie continued. "I'm only going to Colorado for a few weeks!"

"You mean you're not staying?" asked Amy.

"No way! My mother would never allow that! I'm just visiting my dad, and I'll take lessons at the rink in Denver while I'm there!"

The girls looked at one another and grinned. Then they all started laughing over the misunderstanding. Kristen was glad Jamie wasn't leaving for good.

As she tackled the oversized fudge sundae, Kristen thought about all that had happened in the last couple of months. Nothing had turned out the way she expected, but God had helped her through it all. And Kristen knew she could trust Him to help her with all that was to come.